The High Cost Of Victory
A Novel of the Empyrean Republic
By Matt Kirkby

1 - Gathering Clouds

"I fear for our world."

"Nonsense, Duncan." Paladin Jergen chuckled at his aide's concern. "There is nothing to fear." He inhaled deeply from the incense burning in the corner. The gold-flecked marble statue was of a grinning cherub, holding the incense in its cupped hands, the smoke wreathing its face.

"The talk in the streets is all about the growing Separatist movement."

"The talk will never amount to anything other than that. The common folk are content with my rule and we can ignore anything else said. Discontented off-worlders mostly just attempting to stir up troubles here. Ignore them and they will soon fade away into the quiet."

"Are you so certain?"

Jergen looked shocked by the very question. His mouth worked for a few moments before any sounds emerged. "The Republic has stood strong and proud for millennia. Its united strength has fought off aggressors before without defeat." The Republic stood proud and invulnerable, a mighty oak immune to the axes wielded by its independent neighbours. "How can you believe it will fall so easily?"

Duncan shook his own head. "How can it stand if its own citizens despise it?"

"The laws and traditions of society hold us together. We will not falter in our duty. We must strive to improve the Republic so that our descendants will prosper and improve it even more."

"So you say."

"Of course I say."

Duncan shook his head. "My convoy has an escort, old friend. The R.J.D. sent armed warships to escort our freighters through several systems where mercenary forces are trying to prevent trade."

"Prevent trade?" Jergen shook his head at the unpleasant thought. "The trade routes are all recognized as being free space. Neutral space. No one should be in danger travelling on them." After a moment, he grunted. "Aside from the odd pirate band or two I suppose—there are always going to be some disgruntled troublemakers—but most of the galaxy is safe. The laws are all enforced. The Senate has passed several bills about these matters. I was present on Metropolis two or three years ago for one such bill. Bringing the Toraxus Sector under the direct supervision of Judicial Department patrols. Increased several of the local taxes I recall."

"It did indeed." Duncan nodded. "That particular bill tripled some of the import/export customs duties."

Jergen's cheeks paled. "We take a small percentage of those duties which are shared via the Senate-approved budget. I invested most of this world's share into the arts program."

"Well, Paladin, several systems in the Toraxus Sector are now declaring embargoes as a protest against the new taxation laws. They are actually threatening to open fire on freighters passing through those star systems."

Jergen rubbed at his chin. "I can see how some might desire said taxes to be less, or even forgotten, but using armed force to make their demands?" He sounded horrified by the idea. "Are things out there truly that bad?"

"Yes, Paladin, things *are* truly that bad."

"I had no idea."

Duncan said nothing.

Jergen sighed at the unspoken rebuke. He smoothed out the front of his tunic. "I know, I know. I should venture off-world more often." At his age, he disliked space travel. "It is just so hard to find the time."

Duncan nodded. "I know your feelings about space travel." The Paladin had only taken two journeys to the capitol...once after his investiture and once for the funeral of President Kalvalkas.

"You should return to Metropolis. Perhaps you can speak with the Senate and convince them as to how poorly their new laws are being accepted among the outer sectors."

"The Senate does not care."

"They must care! That is their job after all."

"They do not. They are overworked and understaffed in key areas." Perversely, other departments tended towards *over*-staffing. "The weight of millennia tends to make any efforts at change and adaptation to take longer and longer."

"I see."

"The moneys raised through these taxes are making the senators rich."

"Bribery?"

"Not any more than usual." Bribery and corruption were a given in any political system. "Funds raised through taxation are being routed towards various worlds and sectors. Politicians are using those funds to profit their friends and homes. A new factory here, a generous subsidy there. The economy is being perverted to fuel this profit-sharing."

"Taxes are necessary to keep the wheels of government turning." He chewed guiltily at his lip for a moment. "Like the new arts programs I was funding."

"I grant you that, Paladin, but these funds are in the billions of credits. Entire sectors are turning over a substantial portion of their resources and a handful of core worlds are growing wealthy while other outer worlds starve."

"What can we do?"

"Nothing I fear."

Jergen frowned to hear his friend so despondent. "It's an election year. Perhaps when there is some new blood in the Senate..."

"That will not matter. One new senator or another cannot change the flow of history. The bulk of the Senate remains the same. Too many old families entrenched in the political structure. We cannot hope to break such a firm stranglehold...not without a major upheaval."

"Then what do you suggest I do?" Jergen held his arms open, his rich robes falling away from his hands. "I am the leader of my people. I must do what I can to safeguard them. What would you have me do?" he asked sadly.

Duncan shook his head. "I wish that I had a simple answer for you."

"I could attempt to negotiate a settlement between Toraxus and Metropolis."

"Too little, I fear, too late."

"You cannot mean that it will come to war."

"It might."

"It cannot." Jergen felt weak and looked about him for a chair. "There hasn't been a major interstellar war in centuries." He wasn't even certain the Republic could field a unified army/navy. Member worlds and states tended to field their own local militias and police forces to deal with pirates and rogues. "Can the Judicial Department even prosecute a war?"

"No one knows."

"Then why don't they see this for the madness that it is?"

"Because it has gone too far." Duncan shook his head. "We are old men, Jergen. Our day is passing and the younger generation must forge their own path."

"But this path will lead to suffering." A war was nothing to be taken lightly. He eyes rested on the statue...it seemed to be leering at him now, the smoke curling around its features as if it was standing on a smoking battlefield, laughing at the ruins of civilization at its feet.

"I see nothing that we can do. A war is coming and whether the Republic stands or falls will up for the younger generation to decide."

Final Chances

"We are doing our best, Senator."

"Your best is simply not good enough." Stre'vex shook his head in the Human fashion. "This entire situation is intolerable."

"The protestors are not threatening your person."

"No, but they are blocking the path to the spaceport." He squinted at some of the signs, unsuccessfully attempting to decipher the alien scribbling. "Disperse them."

"That is not within our mandate at this time."

Stre'vex drew himself to his full height. "I am a legally appointed representative of Colm'Torket," he announced in his most authorative voice. "I *demand* that you remove those protestors."

The attaché shrugged. "Republic law grants them the right to protest. If they venture onto private property, then they can and will be removed. In the meantime, they have the right to demonstrate their thoughts."

"I see." The senator turned away.

The attaché only shrugged. "I can do nothing at this time."

"Then you are of little use to me."

David poured drinks then vanished from the office.

Stre'vex checked his finger claws. "You had a safe flight?"

"Yes." No'brin managed to keep his crest scales from rising in an involuntary sign of aggression as he stared at the senator. "Until I landed that is."

"The Humans refuse to disperse the protestors." Stre'vix snapped his fangs together. "I have offered many protests but they will do nothing until the rabble enter the spaceport proper."

"Perhaps an incident can be arranged."

"Or manufactured?"

No'brin wrinkled his muzzle. "For a sufficient amount of credits, Humans will sell their own offspring."

Stre'vex shuddered.

"I see that your time on this barren world has not corrupted you."

"I am still a proud child of Colm'Torket. I am Cren'tha. I serve as I am called upon to serve." He kept his voice cold. Questioning the boundaries of his honor was dangerous, even for a clan-brother.

"Even if such service requires dealing with Humans?"

"Even then. I am Cren'tha," he repeated.

"Good. The Elders feared that you had become soft."

"Oh?"

"You have a Human servant."

"The attaché was given to me by the Senate. I have been unable to replace him...as yet."

"Excuses."

"Inefficient Human bureaucrats." Humans clogged the hidden workings of the government. They were everywhere...like vermin. "The only replacement offered thus far was a *Chern'otha*."

No'brin shuddered at the thought.

"I would have no carrion eater working in my office so I am stuck with this Human." Stre'vex offered a partial shrug. "He is efficient at least."

"Perhaps the Elders should send others from the home warrens to assist you."

Stre'vex managed to keep his crest scales from standing erect, but only just barely. "What do the Elders want of me?" On this world, *he* wielded more power than the Clan Elders.

"The new taxation law must be changed. It affects our shipyards."

"I know that."

No'brin said nothing.

"As do you," Strevex challenged. "We must take steps to alter the flow of fate else...." He took a long drink from his cup. The fermented *jerpa* milk burned nicely as it pooled within his second stomach.

"Or else?"

"Or else our civilisation will tear itself apart in an orgy of violence."

"So you claim."

"You disagree?"

"I have seen no proof of any such threat."

"You will soon."

"More protests?"

"Some."

"I will do what I can, but the Senate is burdened with dead weight. Too many bureaucrats. Too many mewling children playing at politics. It needs to be culled."

"In time perhaps we will oversee such a culling."

Stre'vex bared his fangs in a predator's smile. "I would relish such a culling." Metropolis would be more tolerable if it housed billions fewer Humans. "The workings of the government would be swifter should their ranks be thinned."

"The time will come. The Elder have seen it in their fire-visions."

"Then *our* time will come?"

"Yes."

"It will be good to see the Humans gone." The two Cren'tha laughed.

"I want you to contact BuShips. I wish to dine with Administrator Goszka."

David nodded politely as he entered the data onto his computer pad. "As you wish, Senator."

"There is much business to discuss."

"I am sure there is."

"Then why do you stand there?"

"Because you are going to be occupied this evening...and for all evenings to come."

Stre'vex turned away from his computer monitor with a puzzled twist to his muzzle.

David drew a small pistol from inside his jacket. "For the future," he proclaimed as he pulled the trigger.

Stre'vex looked down at the smoking hole in his senatorial robe.

David shook his head. "It's for the best," he said softly as the senator crumpled to the carpets.

ILL TIDINGS

Sarah Douglas strode through the corridor, her booted feet clicking loudly on the deck-plates.

"Good morning, Sarah."

"Is it?" she asked as the other officer fell into step with her.

"Well, seeing as we haven't arrived on duty yet and thus have not viewed the latest data, we can assume that it's a good morning."

"You're impossible, Kirk."

"I try to be." He offered her a playful smile. "Why be depressed at this hour?" He ran a hand through his blond hair. It was slightly longer than strict regulations, but shorter than natives of his home world usually wore their hair.

"Because you know what is happening!" Sarah heard the irritation in her voice and tried to calm herself. "You know what's at stake. Disturbances are spreading daily. Riots, protests, rumours of rebellion. Out there, right now...."

"And Flaming Sword is far away from any of the current flash-points."

"The current ones," she agreed. "What about ones we don't know about?"

"I don't think Chalice is likely to erupt in rebellion."

"Can we take that chance?"

Kirk laughed. "This is a sector capitol," he reminded her. "It's not going to rebel against the Republic. Not with half the Fleet currently in orbit."

Sarah sighed. "I worry too much."

"The Separatists aren't everywhere. It's still just a few disgruntled worlds in the outer territories."

"There are protests on Metropolis."

"There are how many billion inhabitants on the capital?" Kirk countered. The last census was as much guesswork as actual fact. "How many billions of visitors and tourists and students and ships on layovers. I would be far more surprised if there were *not* protests of some kind." Kirk held his hand towards the security scanner and the hatch opened.

Sarah allowed her own hand to be scanned before she followed him into the computer centre.

"Good morning, Lieutenant."

"Good morning, Lieutenant." Sarah replied. "I relieve you."

"I stand relieved."

"Enjoy your off-time, Alexis."

"I'll try, Kirk." The other woman waved. "Nothing interesting yet. Just a few routine reports from the Brittany system."

"Okay."

Alexis left and the hatch closed behind her.

"Now that I have you alone—"

"Kirk!"

"Yes?"

"This is hardly the time."

"I think it's the perfect time." He smiled. "No one is likely to interrupt us after all. I've got you locked in here with me." He walked towards her. "I love having this shift with you."

"You're impossible!"

"So you keep saying."

A computer beeped softly.

Sarah broke eye contact with Kirk. "A report just got logged."

"It can wait."

"No, it can't."

"You are too devoted to duty," Kirk protested half-heartedly as she pulled away from him.

"It's a failing of mine." Pulling her eyes away from him, she moved to the console and typed in her password. "Oh my god!"

"What is it? What's wrong?" All trace of humour was gone from Kirk's voice as he hurried to her side.

"A flash transmission from Brittany. The Separatists have declared war on the Republic!"

* * *

Sarah Douglas felt nervous as she stepped into the commander's office. This was not an area of Flaming Sword Anchorage that she was used to visiting. Even the size of the office was far removed from the areas she normally worked in. It was a spacious one with several large view ports giving a fine view of the station's curved bulk and of the white-flecked green and blue planet. The station's commanding officer sat behind a large and ornately carved wooden desk.

"Does that conclude your report, Lieutenant?"

"Yes, Admiral Makuna." She kept her voice calm. *A wooden desk,* she thought idly. *A desk like that is expensive, more so than a space station would normally carry.* Mass and weight were at a premium after all; most inhabitants made do with low-mass furnishings. *Obviously the Admiral likes to flaunt his importance in less than obvious ways.*

"Things are growing ever more tense. This could be the spark that ignites a full-fledged war."

"I hope not."

"Hopes may not carry much weight at the moment." Nom Makuna shook his head. "I have been in contact with other elements of the Fleet, and with the Admiralty. The situation is worse that publicly known. Once word about Brittany gets out, there will be no stopping the rumours."

And rumours tend to travel faster than ships with hyperdrives. "What about the Senate?"

"Deadlocked. Pro-unity factions and the more militant Separatists are bickering and tying up the machinery of government. It looks like a deliberate effort by some Senators to disrupt the Senate from responding effectively to the declaration of war."

That brought her back to reality. "What are your orders, Admiral?"

He nodded crisply to her. "Continue to monitor the reports. I want to know if any further fighting erupts."

"Of course, Admiral."

"I expect the JDF to move quickly and try to contain the violence. The officers on the scene will do all that they can of course." Makuna's voice was grim. "But if matters remain unchanged, then Brittany will only be the first world to burn."

The Ducks Shoot Back

"No word from Sector Commander yet?"

"Negative, Captain."

"It's been nearly two days since we heard about the rebellion on Brittany. Surely the Admiralty must have plans to launch a counterattack." Danielle Helmer paced across the bridge. "This is intolerable."

"We can do little more than wait for the Senate to come up with a decision."

"That could take an eon or longer." Danielle sighed. "Any word from the planetary governor?"

"He is still locked in debate with the Council."

"How long does it take to decide whether you are loyal or not?" Danielle demanded. "Either he is still loyal to the Republic, or else he's a traitor."

"If he turns traitor, there is the small matter of a fleet in orbit." Jorgos ruffled his fur, a sign of irritation with his species, as he considered her question. "A few corvettes are sufficient to level his cities from orbit."

"The Judicials would never sanction an orbital bombardment!" She was horrified by the mere idea. "That would violate how many unwritten rules of warfare?"

"Enough that no one *Human* wants to consider the possibility."

"Jorgos, you are vicious."

The Shrevrex bared his fangs at the perceived compliment.

The deck lurched and threw the senior officers from the feet.

"Report!" Danielle shouted over the sudden wail of klaxons.

"Incoming fire!" someone shouted back. "Deflector screens up!"

"From who?"

"The defence grid is targeting us," Jorgos snarled from his station. "Multiple impacts on all aft decks. Heavy damage to the aft superstructure." Taken completely by surprise, it was a miracle the ship hadn't been destroyed in the first volley.

"Battle stations!" New alarms began to wail. "Contact SpaceGuard One. What the hell is going on?"

"No response, Captain."

"Evasive manoeuvres. Get us away from SG-One." Danielle hastily attempted to think. "A malfunction of some kind?" she wondered. "Or else this is cold betrayal."

"*Kalahari Sunset* has been destroyed."

"Betrayal," Jorgos hissed. "Because *Baldrock Desert* is not taking fire at all. I am detecting its targeting system though...locking onto us."

"Go evasive! Full power to engines." The Judicials *had* been betrayed all right. "Comm, send a report to Sector Command. Priority Alpha-Red."

"*Baldrock* is moving in pursuit."

"We're an even match for that corvette," Danielle reminded her crew. "We can beat them." Assuming that her already battered ship could hold out. "Taken by surprise, this betrayal must be avenged."

* * *

"The Fifth Star Lancers are advancing towards the capitol."

Phil Agnew nodded. "The defences?"

"The militia is digging in, but I don't know if we're going to be able to stop the Lancers short of the capitol. If we fail, the civilian casualties could, no *will*, be horrendous."

"So it's up to us to stop them?"

"Your pilots are the only ones who can save us."

"No pressure then."

Susan smiled weakly. "None at all."

"You do realise," Phil pointed out, "that if your allies had been able to seize control of SG-One or the *Baffin Shield* itself, then none of this would be necessary?"

"The *Shield* was further out of weapons' range than expected. Her captain was too firmly in control of the crew for us to subvert her."

"So a loyalist corvette escaped into the asteroid field and drew off your sole loyal warship." Thus allowing a window for a Judicial unit to land on the world and strike at the capital city.

"The gunnery crews onboard SG-One have been chastised."

"I should hope so."

"In the meantime, the Lancers are closing. Can you deal with them, Flight Commander?"

"No problem." Phil offered a salute. "We'll launch immediately. The Lancers won't know hit them."

* * *

"Begin the attack run." Phil smiled to himself as the pull of the engine thrust pushed him against the restraints holding him in his chair. "Coming up on the initial target."

"*No challenge here*," one of his pilots complained. "*Just like shooting ducks from behind a hunting blind, Captain. It's just a munitions dump. One shot and the whole place will go up in a fireball.*"

"One stray shot and you could go up in that fireball." Phil checked his displays. "We're expecting resistance."

"*I'll believe that when I—*"

"Strike Three? What were you saying, Three" Phil changed frequencies. "Strike Three respond please?" The crackle of static was loud in his eardrums. "Tighten up, Two."

"*Copy that.*"

Sensors began chiming. "We're being pinged." The Lancers had set up defences after all. "Sometimes the ducks shoot back," he muttered.

Surrounded By The Conflagration

"Metropolis is just ahead, my Prince."

"Thank you, Captain." Even resting in his personal cabin, Saint-Jamis had felt his yacht, *Pacifist's Dream*, leave hyperspace. He glanced at a monitor relaying a visual from a camera mounted on the external hull.

The Republic's most important planet was a fairly average-sized terrestrial world. Blue oceans covered three quarters of the surface, with one large continent and two smaller ones providing living space. The largest continent was completely covered by a single immense city. Currently on the planet's night side, it was plainly visible from orbit as a sprawling mass of light.

He reached for the intercom again. "How long until we enter orbit?"

"About fifteen minutes."

Given the sheer number of ships and vessels around the capital, that would be a fast trip in. "Use the transponder to get a priority vector."

"As you command, my Prince."

The transponder would identify the *Dreams* as a senatorial vessel and clear a path through the ship lanes—the satellite buoys would do their best to keep the traffic lanes clear—which would speed up the voyage. Normally Saint-Jamis disliked using such privilege, but the summons to the emergency session could not be ignored. *Not with the level of fighting erupting throughout the galaxy*, he thought grimly. "How did it come to this?" he mused aloud.

On the bright side, the diplomatic transponder warned off customs officials and also disarmed the local defence grid. Needless to say, Metropolis possessed one of the most powerful defence grids in the galaxy, more than capable of holding off an attacking fleet long enough for reinforcements to arrive from other systems. The standing garrison of warships and fighters always numbered in the hundreds as well.

Starlight glinted off a frigate—the *Suzanne Hayes*, he thought—also moving towards Metropolis.

The Arcadian Cluster has no need of such raw firepower to protect itself, he thought. *His world had disarmed its armies and battle fleets long ago. We have peace...why can't the rest of the galaxy learn to despise war as we do?* That question had no easy answer, he feared.

"We are cleared for landing at NorthPort, my Prince."

"Good." Only a fraction of the ships that entered the system ever received landing clearance. Most had to dock at one of the six SpaceGuard fortresses or one of the other dozen civilian-operated space stations and take registered shuttles down to the planet's surface. The combination of security and old bureaucracy disturbed him. But there would just be too many ships launching and landing to be safe otherwise, he reminded himself. Perhaps Metropolis is simply too small to be a worthy capital for the Republic. *Is that part of the problem currently plaguing us?*

> SpaceGuard Two was now on visual, orbiting above the planet's north pole. One of the huge fortresses orbited at each pole and four others were spaced around the equator. Each heavily armed station held numerous fighter squadrons to protect the planet from attack, as well as serving as docking ports for incoming traffic.

* * *

The view from the tower was stunning. Fancifully shaped towers rose towards the sky, steel and glass shining in the sunlight. Saint-Jamis felt himself impressed. *It is a worthy rival to Arcadia,* he thought. *Though my home world is still prettier. This may look like some fairytale city, but it is artificial. It lacks a soul.*

Saint-Jamis turned and stepped through the door into the Celestial Judicial Courthouse proper. His private landing platform—another senatorial perk—was situated midway up one of the numerous towers. The former Celestial Judicial Courthouse—now the Strategic Military Operations Centre—was crowded. Although the complex was vast, extending far underground as well as up into the towers, it was still crowded. Many of the upper domed levels and towers were still being used for the debate of law, but the more-secure underground warrens had been given over to the demands of the War.

The threat of war, Saint-Jamis thought sadly, *has consumed all thoughts for years. Now it has erupted into open conflict and no one knows how to deal with it. We tried to avoid violence...but too few are interested in talking and too many are interested in fighting.*

Saint-Jamis paused in one huge chamber. A huge holomap was hovering in the air. It seemed detailed enough to show every star in the galaxy. Most of the worlds portrayed by floating lights glowed a comforting green, but the red of rebellion and war glared balefully from too many places. "How did it come to this?" His words went unnoticed by the bureaucrats and officers passing by.

"Welcome to Metropolis, Captain."

Hearing that strong tone, Saint-Jamis turned his head. President Tiresias was standing a few metres away, talking with two military officers. The President of the Republic was a middle-aged Human, dressed in fashionable clothing. His modest-looking green shirt and navy blue pants would not have been out of place on any of a hundred worlds. *Now there is a man who knows the minds of the common folk. He does not stand too far above the people he rules.*

"It is a pleasure to meet you," the President continued to the military officer. "I wish that it could have been under better circumstance." Lines had creased his face, visible proof that the recent outbreak of war was ageing him. "These are trying times for our once-great Republic."

"Sir, I am confident that the Judicial For—I mean the Illustrious Army will stand behind you."

"Much of it does."

"The Separatists don't know what they are doing with this revolt."

"They seek chaos." Tiresias kept his voice steady, but his tone rose steadily in volume. "Many of the other races are jealous of humanity's great wealth and stability. They want to see us humbled. Some wish to see us extinct. Even our fellow Humans are not immune to corruption, falling to the seductive worship of alien gods or the lure of forbidden vices." President Tiresias sighed. "I have done what I can to change the corruption within the Senate, but I am only one man dealing with the legacy of generations of decay and neglect."

"You have my complete support."

"Thank you." Tiresias took Girndt's hand in a firm handshake. "I must go. We will talk again."

Watching Tiresias leave, Saint-Jamis wandered towards a computer console. "What is the latest news?" he demanded.

An officer turned towards him. "Senator," he said after noting the man's identicard.

"What is the latest news from the hot spots?" Saint-Jamis pressed.

"Which ones do you want?" The man shrugged. He knew that this senator was cleared for all levels of information. "Separatist forces have been sighted massing near Bix'tai, placing them within strike range of half a dozen sectors with at least twenty strategic targets. The Tenth Fleet is assembling in the Dadelaus System—which holds the main sector command hub for most of our coreward border—as well being an hour travel-time away from the Cirroc supply depot."

Saint-Jamis shook his head grimly. "The Republic lacks the strength to defend every world."

"The Separatists have many more ships than we had anticipated."

"Defectors and mutinies?"

"For the most part. The secession of the Tairanians didn't help matters any." The officer paused, as if uncertain whether he should continue. "Arcadia is within their strike range."

"You think that my home world is in danger, Colonel?"

"It might be."

"Arcadia is a peaceful world. We have no standing armies, no weapon factories, and no warship supply depots. We are hardly a strategic target to anyone."

"You're weak."

"We are a peaceful people. The violence of our ancestors is buried in the past." *Aside from a handful of citizens who joined the Republic Judicial Forces that is.* "The Cluster is a place of peace, an island of tranquility in a sea of turmoil."

"How poetic." The man sounded unimpressed.

"What else can you tell me?"

"I've heard that Admiral Prancing Deer is taking command of the Fifth Fleet. He plans to move against the Syndicate before it becomes a serious threat to our borders."

"He's an honourable man. Perhaps he can come to terms with the Mojave Syndicate."

"If not, he'll have the firepower to crush it."

Saint-Jamis winced.

* * *

"Another trip? But you've only just returned from Metropolis? Scarcely a week has passed."

Saint-Jamis smiled at his wife. "I am summoned to another emergency session of the Senate."

"This damnable war."

"I must attend. I am the voice of reason."

"I know, dear." Yvonne smiled as the evening breeze blew through the window of the bedroom. "But why must it be tonight?" she asked.

"My shuttle leaves in the morning. We have this night."

"At least we have that."

"We'll have all of time," Saint-Jamis told her. "Arcadia is of no importance to the war. We're quite safe here."

Holding The Line

"Move out."

Ian James checked his displays as the *Onslaught* rumbled forward. His tank mounted some of the heaviest layers of crystal-steel armour available. Three lasers were mounted on the main turret and they began to track incoming targets.

"Looks like three, maybe four *Imps*."

"Light targets then." But fast ones. Those hovertanks were infernally quick, zipping about the battlefield and stinging their foes to death with stabbing beams from their single laser. "Hit them as best you can."

"Targeting the centre one." The gunner checked his sights. "Hold us steady, Mike."

"You got it, Ian." The driver held the tank on a slow rate of approach. "We can weather a few of their hits without even noticing scratches in the armour."

"I know that. Do they?"

The *Imps* were getting closer.

"Just a bit closer...firing now!"

The trio of lasers stabbed out and the crimson beams burned into one of the light tanks. The tank tilted as armour was vaporised and the hover jets attempted to compensate. The formation sundered as the *Imps* scattered. The damaged one tried to turn away but its former speed was now absent.

"Perfect."

"Good shooting."

"I thought so." Ian checked the sights again. "This should finish him." He fired again and the lasers stabbed deep into the hovertank's vitals. The small tank exploded.

"Where'd the others go?"

"No idea."

"Nothing on my screens."

"Maybe they fled."

"I doubt that."

"So do I."

"Head for the ridge. We need to be able to overlook the star port." Helmer-Rasul Munitions maintained a private landing field for their factory complex. It was mostly underground—for security reasons—but the landing field was open to the surface. If the Separatists were able to secure the port, they could interdict the flow of munitions off-world. "Get us to flank speed."

Mike shook his head. "We don't do flank speed. We crawl."

Scorpion's Nest

"Republican troops on approach."

"We'll be ready for them." Colonel Bates cut the transmission and then studied the various displays on her tank's consoles with a frown. The Republican armoured column was advancing towards the pass and only her company of tanks could stop the advance. *We're only expected to slow their advance,* she thought grimly. *The Duke doesn't think we can stop them, despite our best efforts. We're just a sacrificial ploy...sent out here to buy time for the real defenders with our lives. But we'll show them.*

"Colonel, we estimate ten minutes to contact."

She nodded to her crew. "We're ready for them."

"I hope so."

"If this fails, can we get our money back from CMD?"

Bates smiled. The twelve tanks of her company were *Scorpions.* Cameron Metal Works had built cheap thirty ton tanks for several planets in the Caliban Sector. Only five of those tons were amour plating...though the autocannon that made up each tank's main armament should hopefully be able to destroy any enemy unit before *it* could destroy the *Scorpion.*

"Incoming!"

"Identify them!" Bates ordered.

"Looks like three twelve *Furies,* six *Centipedes*...three *Thumpers.*"

Bates cursed softly. The seventy ton *Thumpers* were little threat to her ambush...their main armament was a HammerFist artillery piece designed to bombard stationary targets or fortifications. *Like the capitol?* "We hit the *Furies* first, leave the *Thumpers* for the last." Those eighty ton tanks were the more serious threat with a large laser and two heavy machine guns. The *Centipedes* were practically unarmed, but carried two or three squads of infantry.

"Aye, Colonel." The comm-tech hastily sent the orders to the rest of the company, using line-of-sight laser links to prevent the transmission from being traced or detected.

The lead Republican tanks moved towards the widest patch of open ground. They looked tough, with sloped armour and gleaming insignias freshly painted.

"Now for the strike," Bates said softly. "Attack!" she ordered.

The autocannons opened fire and depleted ore slugs began pounding into the lead tanks.

The 'Scorpion's Nest' was a fine tactical innovation. The defenders had hidden their tanks amongst rocks and boulders, relying on the metallic ores in the area to mask their own machines from detection. Now they struck from ambush and the Republicans reeled.

The combined fire of the Scorpion company struck the leading pair of Furies. Armour crumpled beneath the barrage and both tanks halted with smoke billowing from their torn hulls.

One *Thumper*, near the back of the formation, was hit by a stray shot—one crew had apparently disobeyed orders and targeted the mobile artillery piece—and its magazine detonated, destroying the vehicle and throwing the Republicans into further chaos.

"Infantry is deploying!"

"Take them out!" Bates ordered. The infantry was a distraction from the real threat, but she couldn't allow those soldiers to penetrate her own ranks. Even handheld weapons and grenades could threaten her tanks in time. Luckily, in addition to the autocannons, the *Scorpions* also mounted normal machine guns. The hail of bullets sent the surviving Republicans diving for cover.

Autocannon bursts struck at two of the *Centipedes* who had not yet unloaded their cargo and both APCs blew up in powerful fireballs.

Bates felt a twinge of guilt at the deaths of those soldiers. *Killed before they even knew they were under attack.* But this was war and she would not see her world dominated by the corrupt Republic any longer. *All we want is to be left alone,* she thought. *If the Republic accepted that, then none of those men would have had to die today.*

Her *Scorpion* rocked as enemy fire struck its hull.

"We're holding, but we're taking a pounding here."

"Do your best. Gunner, take out another tank."

"The Duke acknowledges our attack. He reports he has no units in position to support us at this time."

Bates accepted the report with a nod. "We don't need any help," she grunted as she flipped through the visual data being transmitted from her recon team. "The Republicans are on the run!" she crowed.

"We held them?"

"Yes, Lieutenant, we held them." She watched two *Centipedes* and one *Thumper* pulling back. Only two *Furies* were still moving, providing cover fire for their allies. "We held them."

"I have casualty reports incoming."

"Do you wish to pursue, Colonel?"

"Send me the casualty list." Bates hastily checked the damage report. "No, we don't have the strength to pursue." Seven of her *Scorpions* were little more than burning scrap metal, with their crews burned alive no doubt, and three more were badly damaged. "I have two combat-effective units," she said grimly. "If we're unlucky, we might be able to catch up with the Republicans."

The comm-tech nodded. "That would be bad thing, Colonel."

"We hold position," she said. "Our orders are to hold the pass. And by god, we're going to do just that."

"I can't wait to see the Duke's expression when he hears that we managed to hold the pass."

Bates smiled. "It should be memorable."

The High Cost Of Victory

"Withdrawing, the Republican vessel is."

"No choice have they." First Talon Keop watched as the battered frigate pulled away from Lourdes orbit and began to head out-system at the best speed it could manage.

"Pursue them?"

"Let them go." The battle was won and he forced his racing hearts to slow the rate of their beating. Adrenaline drained from his blood. "Damage report?"

"Destroyed two brigantines were, one damaged. Destroyed also almost a hundred PreyDroids."

"Caused such damage did one frigate? Fight well these Republicans do." Keop was worried...a full-scale war could prove most costly under such conditions should one erupt.

"Infected the ecosystem is. Useless to the Humans Lourdes will now be."

"Polluted the world is, but useless it is not." Keop flicked his tail as he considered the toxins released into the atmosphere during the earlier fighting. "Unaffected we are. Ours this world now is." A flush caused his scales to darken. "Weaker, the mammals are."

"Respond will they? Bio-chem of their own?"

"Perhaps. No Humans will reach our nests. Too strong are we."

"Gamble on this we do."

"The Republic crumbles. Against one world, strong they are. Against so many, they lack strength."

"Share your confidence I do not."

"Strike we must. Off-balance the Republicans kept must be." Keop smiled. "A raid into the Arcadian Cluster would suffice for a fresh strike."

"Destroy us it would. Lack the strength for such an attack we do."

"Arcadia crippled already is. The shipyards only remain."

"Cherbourg?"

"Aye."

"A bold move indeed."

"Destroy the shipyards and remove a threat we can."

"Unsure of this strategy I am."

"Do what we can we will."

Whatever The Cost

Lord Mauer stared at the planet as his ship made its approach. *Metropolis*, he thought, *how beautiful you are.* The planet was a fairly average-sized terrestrial world with blue oceans covering three quarters of the surface and one large continent and two smaller ones providing living space for billions of inhabitants. The largest continent was completely covered by a single immense city.

"We are approaching orbit."

He nodded to the captain. "Transmit our clearance codes," he ordered. "We have priority clearance."

"As you say, my Lord." The captain sounded nervous. Understandable, of course, for the planet known galaxy-wide as Metropolis possessed one of the most powerful defence grids in the galaxy, more than capable of holding off an attacking fleet long enough for reinforcements to arrive from other systems. The standing garrison consisted of scores of warships and hundreds of starfighters. Six massive SpaceGuard space stations orbited Metropolis—one over each pole and four spaced around the equator. With the outbreak of war, security had increased and the local defenders had already opened fire on two transports that had been slow to transmit their transponder beacon and security codes.

"I believe that the Empyrean Republic has served its time," President Tiresias calmly said to his companion as they paced along a balcony. The view of the Metropolis cityscape was stunning. Fairy-tale architecture had long been the standard for construction giving the city a unique beauty. "The unity which once bound our worlds together has been lost...perhaps forever."

"The weak have fallen and dragged the rest of us down," Mauer growled. "We must be strong if we are going to rebuild." His dark cloak swirled around him as he paced with a strong military-style bearing.

"My thoughts exactly." Tiresias was dressed in rich blues and greens, and his gait was more mincing. He was not a warrior, nor did he possess military training. *I am a politician. My place is guiding people, not fighting with them.*

"The Senate is divided."

"The Senate has always been divided. A legacy from its past. Only rarely does an outside threat unite the various member-states into acting in unison." *A problem I have yet to completely overcome.* "I am surprised they managed to agree that we must go to war in the first place. I doubt they will see the need which forces us to act in a harsh manner."

"Humanity must survive."

"Yes, *Humanity* must survive," Tiresias agreed. "But can it? The lure of alien vices seduces many of our citizens. The siren song of alien gods. The alluring scent of alien drugs. The seductive smiles of alien whores." He shook his head. "Much of our star fleet defected following the initial rebellion...that loss weakens us greatly."

"The traitors will die."

"I wish that I shared your confidence."

"The bulk of the Republic stands with you. The bulk of our worlds and citizens remain loyal. The Security Bureau has pledged itself to you."

"I shall have a new task for you."

"I live only to serve you, Mister President."

Tiresias smiled. "There's been heavy fighting in the Tigress Sector."

"How heavy?"

"The Sigma Supremacy has been skirmishing with loyalist forces for the last three weeks."

Mauer shook his head. "There's nothing of value in that sector."

"There are ten inhabited systems in that sector, but none of them have any strategic importance. Tigress is the only Republic-loyal world in that region. The neighbouring sectors are either independent or else controlled by the Supremacy."

"The Sigmites are deluded if they think they can stand up to the Republic."

"In normal times they would be crushed...but right now we are vulnerable. Our Illustrious Army is scattered across a thousand worlds. And so the Tigress Sector is vulnerable."

"Will you send ships?"

"I have none to spare."

Mauer tilted his head.

"Separatist forces have been raiding the Fokkers-Mitsubishi Starplex."

Mauer cursed softly as he digested that piece of information. "That's one of the largest yards in the galaxy."

The President nodded. "Precisely. You know how vital it is to our military. If we lose control of the Yards..."

"Then we'll lose the Wars."

"I have assigned R.I.M. and the Admiralty to protect the Yards. The Supremacy remains a threat for another sort of operation."

"My talents are at your command."

"I was hoping that you would say that, Lord Mauer."

1 Justification

"I do what I must for our freedom." Star Admiral Chorfa-nak kept his voice calm as the *Dark Majesty* dropped out of hyperspace almost on top of Isis Station.

"The station's weapons are not powered," the sensor officer reported.

"Give them a warning shot."

"Yes, Admiral."

Lasers stabbed out and armour vaporised. The station shuddered under the barrage as one of its cargo bays was blasted opened to vacuum.

"The station's commander is hailing us. He sounds urgent."

"Fire again."

The second barrage was more fearsome than the first and a large section of lights disappeared as power was disrupted throughout the station.

"Weapons systems are powering up."

"We're being targeted!"

"Cripple them."

Ineffectual laser fire from the station's few functional batteries splashed harmlessly against the *Majesty's* deflector screens.

Almost a pretty light show, Chorfa-nak thought. "Target the weapons and disable them."

Most of the gunners tried to obey, though a fairly high percentage of their shots missed their intended targets and exploded against the station's hull.

"Multiple breaches across the superstructure. Power levels are dropping."

"I think we've crippled them, Admiral."

"Cease fire." *I have no desire to make this a senseless slaughter of innocents.* Enough that he had to launch the attack in the first place. "I will accept the surrender of Isis Station now."

"Will this raid work, Admiral?"

"It had better. We're trying to draw off defenders so the real attack will succeed." He sighed. "I would rather be involved in the real fighting than waste my time here."

"Agreed."

No World An Island

"The League has been operating on a fairly independent course for centuries. These worlds were first colonized by citizens attempting to leave behind the stranglehold of a galaxy-wide bureaucracy."

"I understand that, Tyran Tsonos, but surely the League cannot be willing to cast aside every aspect of its former glory."

Tsonos looked at the ambassador with a frown. "The Illustrious Army of *your* Republic wages war against a thousand worlds," he said coldly. "Many of which seek only the freedom and right to determine their own fates. The Hellenic League will not continue to support such endeavours."

"Your decision to withhold your annual taxes stands?"

"The League will not pay taxes to a distant government to help fund this war. Nor we will conscript our own citizens to augment its Army of oppression."

"The Senate will not be pleased by this."

Tsonos leaned back in his chair. The throne was carved from a solid block of Olympian marble, which matched the columns holding up the mosaic-covered ceiling. "The Senate is of no concern to us. The League Council has voted on this matter. Our worlds will no longer tolerate the ongoing tyranny of the Senate. We will not allow ourselves to support a government that fails to support the desires of its people."

"The President wishes you to be fully aware of the probable consequences of this decision. He begs you to reconsider."

"I know the consequences, Ambassador." Tsonos sighed heavily as he weighed his options for the last time. *I have no choice left to me...I must do what my people want.* "We all know the consequences of our defiance...and yet that defiance stands. The League refuses to support the Republic...hence we are left with no other choice than to *secede.*"

The Ambassador drew a deep breath. "That's a large step."

"It is the only step."

"The Senate—"

"Remains irrelevant."

"Tyran—Spiros—don't do this."

"Inform President Tiresias and the Senate that as long as their Illustrious Army remains outside of the borders and territory currently held by the League, there will be peace. No League forces will raid, harass, or invade sovereign territory of the Republic. We will not offer military or economic aid to any of the other Separatist systems in their war against the Republic. This is my pledge to you. The League wants only peace and to be left alone." He paused. "Should our territorial borders be breached, then the League *will* defend our worlds with every warship, starfighter, and soldier that we can muster."

"Is that your final decision, Tyran?"

"It is the only one left to me, Ambassador."

The Human drew himself to his full height. "Then I shall take my leave," he announced formally. "Good day."

* * *

"You let him go?"

"What good would it do us to hold the ambassador hostage?" Tsonos shook his head. "One more prisoner would do the League little good and much harm. We do not seek to wage war against the Republic, only to defend what is ours."

General Empey shook his head. "I see your point," he conceeded.

"Good." Tsonos turned back to the servant approaching with a tray of light refreshments. The small terrace overlooked one of the palace gardens and the scent of roses filled the air. The morning sun was bright but a gentle breeze kept the air cool. *A most civilized place for a meeting,* he thought. "What is the status of our military defence?"

"I have sent General Giggins to oversee the defence of Chios. I foresee that world being pivotal in the overall defence of the League."

Tsonos mentally studied a star map in his head. Like any ruler, he tried to keep a general knowledge of how his territory was laid out. "What of Ionia and Thrace?"

"Those worlds, along with Joppa and Lesbos are sources of resources...but the key to holding that area is Chios and the factories situated on that world." Chios was one of the League's most productive industrial worlds. "General Giggins will fortify Chios and the other worlds of that region."

"I suspect that the defences around Athens are strong enough?"

"To hold off the entire Republican Army? No, they're not." Empey shook his head. "There is no possible way that the League alone could hold off the entire Republic should they choose to exert their military might against us." This was a given. "But at the current time, the Republic is divided against itself. It can only commit portions of its military against us. That gives us some slight advantage. Should we desire it, we could move against any of a dozen worlds in nearby sectors and take them easily."

"That would violate my promise of non-aggression."

"I am aware of that, Tyran." Empey did not sound apologetic. "I am also aware that such a strike would prove disastrous in the long run, however successful it proved initially. It would make the League a definite threat and the Senate would be left with no choice but to call for our immediate destruction."

"We must focus on holding our own territory against raids and probes. Should we show weakness, the Republic will move against us."

"Yes, Tyran."

"An expansion of our military is called for."

"How ironic that the very taxes we do not send to Metropolis to arm its Army will instead be spent arming ourselves."

"The universe has a cruel sense of humour." Tsonos turned back to the garden with a sigh.

Practical Vision

"This mining facility is fairly important to the Republic."

"The minerals you mean?" the naval officer asked in a bored voice. "Or the location? I've toured too many worlds in the last few months. All of you claim to be vital to the Republic, and yet none of you truly are. Our resources are stretched thin fighting in the wars and only a few ships can be spared to guard one outer rim planet."

The two bureaucrats exchanged looks. "Trilithium crystal is important to the military," the older man said.

"Vital," the second bureaucrat added.

"But the natives are less than enthusiastic in their labours."

"They are delaying our exports."

"They are threatening the Republic's safety."

"I see. I assume that you tried to bring in off-worlders?"

"We did...but the natives fought back. They claimed we violated their lands—rubbish!"

"Right now work at the major mining pit is impossible due to protests and attacks. Workers cannot leave their quarters without being shot at. Bows and arrows are so primitive, yet they can kill as easily as a slug-thrower."

"I can spare a few days to put down a rebellion." Captain Devalis nodded to himself. "Show me the locations of the major native population centres. I will show you how to end a rebellion."

"Of course. The maps should be uploaded into your systems already."

* * *

"Bring sensors online."

"Ventral weapon batteries standing by, Captain."

"Targets locked?"

"Yes, Sir."

Devalis stood near the windows, staring down at planet slowing rotating below. Such a pretty sphere of green and blue, laced with white clouds. *Very pretty indeed.* "Fire at will."

* * *

Lasers flashed through the clouds.

"Separatist forces are on approach."

"Warn them off."

"No response, Captain."

"Warn them again and lock lasers."

"Locked."

"Fire." Devalis watched the beams flash towards the approaching ships. "Send a distress signal to Metropolis. Request reinforcements."

"We can hold those scum, Captain."

"They'll call in back-up. They want this world so we have to deny it to them." He paused. "Even though it's nearly useless to us both."

* * *

The natives dug.

Armoured marines stood and watched over them with their weapons held in comfortable positions.

"I see that the work is progressing?"

"It is." The administrator nodded. "The crystals are vital to the manufacture of laser emitters and focusing arrays."

Devalis nodded. "I know. I read the briefing."

"The Republic needs those supplies to arm its ships."

The captain shook his head. "We're under a full blockade right now. The Seppies are holding most of the outer system. My ship can't break orbit to engage them without leaving the planet vulnerable."

"I have heard this."

"On the other hand, they can't slip past us to hit the planet without coming into range where we can hit them. And hurt them."

"So you have a stalemate."

"The Fleet will send ships. They have too."

"Yes, when the next shipment is ready to be transported to the shipyards."

"Another few weeks. We'll be fine until then."

"I wish that I shared your confidence."

"What about the natives?"

"What of them?"

"When we depart with the shipment, what will happen to them?"

"They will be protected. There are other mines to dig still."

"And you need these slaves?"

"Volunteers. They are paid for their labours."

Not enough I'm sure. "Why can't you use robots?"

"Too dangerous. The crystals focus and amplify energy...using automated equipment or standard mining machines would be disastrous. Laser cutters would merely feed a chain reaction which might melt the vein into worthless slag or even cause a cascade explosion."

"Which would destroy the entire region?"

"Yes. Hence the manual mining with labourers."

"I don't like this."

"You are not required to like it, Captain, merely to protect this world from the rebels while loyalist companies mine ore to supply the Republic your military serves."

Devalis frowned. "I am returning to my ship."

Nightmares Of Shadow

The strike craft is blazing with fire as its deflector screens failed.

"We've taken hits. Weapons are down."

"Can we outrun them?"

"Not bloody likely, Sir."

"Damn it! I didn't come this far only to be shot down." I eye the displays. "Where did those damned ships come from?"

"No idea, Captain."

"A blind jump through hyperspace to avoid the Seppie fleet massing at Korvan Prime and we still got tracked." The Seppies were closing fast. "Return fire, full barrage." *Maybe we can shoot down some of those war-droids before they fire on us.*

The ship shudders.

"Our engines are hit. We're going to die."

"Head for the planet. Maybe we find a star port."

"I don't even know where we are!" the navigation officer protests. "I have no blazing idea where in the galaxy we are."

"The planet looks like it has an atmosphere." The local star is a dying red dwarf but the planet orbits it closely.

"Droids are coming in for another run."

"Fire at will."

The ship is hit again.

"We're entering the ionosphere too fast. We're going to burn up."

"Braking thrusters!"

"They're not responding."

The heat is intense.

The impact, more so.

Shadowy shapes reach from the mists.

Thunder booms out with deafening volume.

Soft laughter echoes like the wind.

I start awake.

"You made it, Myron," Karl comments.

"Where are we?" I manage to ask.

"Lost on an uncharted planet."

Lightning flares outside the view ports.

"The storm has been raging since we crashed."

"How long was I unconscious?"

"Several hours…maybe a few days. We're not sure. We were all out for at least a little while."

"Great."

"The bridge is wrecked. The main reactor is down—lucky for us it didn't blow."

"Can we call for help?"

"Nope."

"Any good news?"

"We might have gotten a distress signal off before we crashed."

"I see."

Lightning flares and illuminates a dark castle.

Grim and foreboding, it rises from the rocky crags to tower into the sky, as if the mountains have given birth to this structure.

The stones seem to glisten with some moisture.

"It's very dry."

"All this thunder and lightning and never a drop of rain." Karl shook his head. "I don't understand it."

"We must get rain." I look around. There are trees, twisted skeletal forms clawing towards the sky as if in pain.

Dim shapes loom in the mist.

Almost human, but with deformed limbs and twisted faces.

Scales not skin.

Fangs overfilling mouths.

"We are Draalakul," one creature hisses.

"Too long without fresh minds."

"Fresh fears."

"Too long."

The voices hiss and I try to run.

Clan Honour

The corvette descended from the cloudy sky, its hull glowing with the heat of re-entry.

Dark-hulled, with forward swept wings and bristling with openly displayed firepower, it was the craft of a hunter. Even its engines shrieked as they laboured to keep it aloft. It hovered in the air, panels opening and claw-like landing gear emerging slowly into place.

Then it slowly settled onto the landing pad with a soft thud.

The main hatch opened and the crew stepped out.

"A good haul, Vo-druk?"

"Aye, Bes-rak." The burly captain nodded, shaking his head with its mane of horns and baring his fangs.

"How many ships did you hit?"

"Five freighters on this hunt." Netting him almost two dozen slaves. "My status grows here on Home."

"Slaves plus wealth...small wonder the corsairs are strong."

"The prey are weak," Vo-druk snarled. "Weak and divided." Unlike the Gro-jonk Clans.

"The wars rage on...let them squabble."

Several of the slaves were being led off the corvette now. Pale skinned, with a tough of dark fur atop their heads. They were shorter than the Gro-jonk, thinner, and their flat faces were repulsive.

"They look healthy."

"They are. I spaced the weak ones." No point bringing home useless slaves.

* * *

Vo-druk growled as his fangs ripped chunks from the haunch of zreb. *It's freshly slain*, he thought. "A meal worthy of a great hunter."

"You honour the clans."

"I honour me." He licked blood from the tips of his claws.

His mate watched him—as was proper—even though she felt the stirrings of hunger. "The new slaves will serve."

"I trust they will learn their place."

"If not, you will dine upon them."

Vo-druk bared his fangs. "There's little meat on their fragile bones."

"There'll be less when you've worked them awhile."

"They are slaves now. Not ship crews or techs. They exist at my whim."

"You will work them?"

"As I wish."

"You will sell them?"

"No. They live and die as I wish. I no sell to others. Slaves are status and my status grows."

"Gory to the Clan then."

* * *

The mane of horns around the top of his head were a dark mottled colour, as befitted an elder of his advanced years. "You have prospered, Vo-druk."

"My mate has birthed thirty cubs," he boasted. "My house supports forty personal slaves. The Clan is strong."

"Your pride is strong as well."

"I serve."

"Our Clan *is* strong, I grant you that." His yellow eyes narrowed. "The prey are learning hot to fight back. They have destroyed a claw's worth of corsairs in the last moon."

Vo-druk snarled. "From our Clan, Vo-gat?"

"From others. The Bes and the Trig have lost ships."

"Weak Clans."

"They need to rethink their place in the Rankings. Our Clan has the chance to rise...if the hunters are worthy of trying."

"I am. Guide me."

The Elder smiled, baring his own age-yellowed fangs. "A prey-fleet is gathering near Nyx...go there and destroy it. You will gain many slaves from this raid."

"And much status."

"Of course."

Vo'druk laughed. "I hunt!"

"The Clan goes with you."

"Must it?"

"Aye. The risk is great, the honour is greater. Our Clan cannot fail in this!"

* * *

Nyx lay ahead. A barren system, with a small colony or research station of some kind on one moon. No known defences. No significant warship strength. An easy target.

Vo-druk bared his fangs in a silent snarl as his corsair led the pride of the Vo Clan towards their prey.

"There is much signal-spoor in orbit."

"More prey?"

"Many ships."

Vo-druk's mouth gaped wider. "More honour and slaves to be taken." He did not known fear—that emotion had been beaten out of him decades ago by the Clan Elders and other rivals. "Forward, all speed. Rend their flanks with our lasers." He laughed grimly. "Slaughter all who resist."

Vo-druk watched with disbelief as one of his Clan's corsairs blew part under the combined firepower of three other ships. "They dare?"

"Fighters launching."

"Droids."

"They send machines to fight for them. They lack all honour." The prey were barely worthy of taking as slaves. He snorted loudly.

"We're taking hits."

Flashes shimmered beyond the view ports.

"The main warships are moving."

"Return fire."

"More ships than expected. More droids than we thought to see."

Explosions lit space beyond the view ports.

Vo-druk saw his Clan's fleet in ruins. The lives lost were nothing, but the dishonour of this defeat would mar the Clan for decades.

l Song Of The Machine

The bio-ship crouches on the rough cavern floor.

It does not rest on landing pad-legs like our shuttles and small craft. It seems to crouch, as if prepared to spring into movement at a moment's notice.

Is it waiting for something? Is it asleep? Or is it dead? Am I just imagining these things? I give my head a shake. The cavern is no place for me to give into idle daydreams. I, and the rest of my staff, have much work ahead of us.

My technicians installed the light-panels in here after discovering this cavern and their harsh glare has banished all of the former shadows. There is nothing hidden from us.

"This is a grand day for the scientific community."

"Agreed." I nod as I look around the cavern. The rocks are a dull grey, with veins of quartz running through them. The quartz glitters in the work lights. "It is proof that the Republic is not the most advanced civilisation in the universe." My eyes turn back to the ship—it is so hard to look away for any length of time.

"Perhaps. Perhaps not."

"Why do you say that?"

"How do we know that this is not simply something from a member world's lost colony? It could have been buried here and forgotten about. A crash landing."

"I don't think any member-world has the capability to design and build this type of craft." The bio-engineering was far beyond anything even my own advanced world could match. *I've never heard about anything like this before.*

"We need to take samples."

"Do so." I watch my colleagues hurry to set up their equipment. *This ship has been here for centuries, possibly millennia. I don't think we need to rush right now.* It wasn't going anywhere.

The bio-ship's reptilian-like scales shimmer as I run my eyes along the craft's smooth lines. It has been grown to race through space and even at rest, I can almost see it quiver with the urge to fly.

I pace around the ship.

Scientists are working eagerly on this craft, taking samples from the hull—or should I call it *skin*?

"...will advance our knowledge of bio-organic manipulation by centuries."

"I concur. This could open up an entirely new area of..."

I move around to the front of the ship.

An orifice gapes open.

The entry hatch...or a hungry mouth?

I step through, feeling as if the bio-ship has swallowed me whole.

Silly thoughts, I tell myself. Other scientists have entered the ship through that very orifice before me and taken samples from the interior. Nothing happened. The bio-ship remains oblivious to our presence.

Dead.

The interior of the craft is damp, despite the dryness of the cavern, and the air has a smell to it unlike that found on our own sterile ships. Not an unpleasant smell, by any means, but a strange one I cannot quite place despite the feeling of familiarity it has. *Down by the pond where I used to catch frogs,* I think to myself.

I feel an *essence* around me. I can almost hear singing—as absurd as that claim sounds. The song is just too faint to be heard, but it's there.

I look around the craft's interior. It is empty. A roughly oblong space matching the external contours of the bio-ship. No equipment. No machinery. No computer consoles. No displays. "If this is the bridge," I say aloud, "then where does the crew sit to operate it?" There are no chairs. Just empty space.

The greenish-brown wall seems to pulsate hypnotically. I am drawn to touch it. It dimples under my fingers. Warm, soft, not slimy at all though it looks damp. It feels most odd...just like a snake's skin. The warm material ripples along the walls and then it suddenly surges and envelopes my hand up to my wrist. Before I can take any action, before I can even scream, it surges again and envelops my entire body. I try to scream but I can't draw a breath.

The song is louder, calming in its melody.

I struggle to escape, but I cannot move.

Trapped...to be eaten alive!

The song grows louder still. I can understand it now and my desperate struggles slow. The bio-ship is *singing* to *me*, telling me of its nature, of its timeless beauty. There is nothing to fear, just an urge to travel and explore.

It's all clear to me.

The bio-ship sings to me of a long journey through the trackless depths of space. It sings of visiting strange planets which humanity has yet to discover. It sings of sights and colours for which there is no name. It sings of dancing among asteroids and skimming the event horizon of a black hole. It sings of drifting through nebulas and watching the birth of stars. It sings of the meeting of numberless star herds of its fellows.

It sings to me of loneliness.

I want to cry as waves of melancholy sweeps through me.

So alone, the song seems to cry.

I'm with you now, I tell it. *You are no longer alone.*

Joy washes away the sadness.

Pure joy.

I want to weep at the strength of the raw emotion.

Outside, one of my colleagues tries to cut a sample from the hull.

"Stop," I moan, feeling the pain of that cut lance through me. The ship's song is louder, more insistent. *The laser burns!*

"We need a stronger laser," he says, not hearing me.

Oh the pain! The bio-ship cries out.

"Stop!" I scream and energy surges through me, consuming the lab in a ball of fire.

We break through the atmosphere, the warmth of our passage feeling wonderful against my/our skin. We move effortlessly. The cavern is behind us now, left deserted.

I feel a touch of sorrow at the deaths of my former companions, but they hurt us. They had to be stopped.

Now We Prey

"There's another one."

A gunshot rang out.

"You missed."

"Shut up."

Jerome eyed the reptilian beast prowling outside the wall.

"There's too many of them."

"We can hold them off."

Miras shrugged. "So you say. So you hope," she amended. "If the wall is breached…"

"The lasers are too strong for them to pass through." Jerome eyed the steadily-humming pylons. Lasers, set a hand's width or so apart, hummed steadily between the silvery metal. "We're safe enough."

"But how long will the energy supply last?"

"It's solar powered."

"How long will our supplies last? We're not solar powered."

"Long enough."

"We're cut off!" Miras snapped. "The Republic stopped signalling us months ago. We're alone out here."

"The Wars must be trying," Jerome guessed, "but we've not been forgotten. Help will come."

Miras muttered something and turned away.

* * *

"The foragers haven't found much."

"There's not much in the woods to eat." Miras shook her head. "And I fear there is too many *things* out there which wish to eat us."

"So we're going to starve?"

"I hope not."

"Still no response to any of our signals. The Republic is not answering."

"Perhaps we should give up on them."

"And just lay down to die?"

"No, I never said that." Miras blinked all four of her eyes. "The Republic is not the only power in the galaxy."

"The Separatists?"

"There are a lot of them in this region. That is why we were sent here wasn't it? To scout this world as a base for the Illustrious Army? Why not ask the Separatists for help? We want off-world, any place must be better than this!"

A distant howling came from the woods.

"If they want to take this world as a base, I say 'welcome to it'! This world is a nightmare." Nasty animals in the woods, poisonous plants, too much radiation from the local star, just to top the list.

* * *

"Our food supplies are dwindling. I do not think they will last us more than a few more weeks at best."

"We need rescue."

"Or resupply."

"I stand by my earlier idea. Call the Separatists for help."

"No."

* * *

"Food supplies are still dwindling."

"So is the population." Miras allowed scorn to colour her voice. "Do you know how many of our people have died?"

"I am aware that one of the foraging parties is late returning."

"Two days late. No one survives a night beyond the fence."

"I can't help them. I have to defend the camp. Only volunteers went out beyond the fence."

"So only volunteers die? How comforting I find that." She turned and stalked away.

* * *

"What do you see, Miras?"

"The stars." She shrugged. "The forest beyond the fence."

A soft hum sounded.

"What was that?"

"I don't know."

A soft growling hiss sounded.

"It's a draclik."

One of the reptilian beasts was edging towards the fence.

"It can't get through."

Miras gestured. "It has laser scars…it's tried before."

"Then it knows it can't get through the beams."

The draclik raised its head and hissed. Its long fangs glinted.

Miras muttered a quick prayer beneath her breath.

The draclik paced towards the two figures, but reared back as lasers burned into its hide. It screeched with pain.

"I don't like this."

"The fence is holding."

"It's glitching." The metal pylons looked rusted. "The local fungus is eating them."

"Impossible."

"It's happening." Miras gestured. "The fence is collapsing…and once it fails, we're all dead."

"We're already dead," Jerome told her. "The hyper-comm is disabled."

"What?"

"Sabotage."

"Someone doesn't want us to leave."

"Someone wants us dead...and we're not going to be able to do anything about it."

Miras turned back to the draclik pacing beyond the glowing laser beam fence. "So now it's just a matter of time?"

Untouchable

"Republican ships are making a run for the asteroid ring."

"Pursuit course, but watch the danger zones."

"Aye, Captain."

Vertak watched the Republican frigate accelerating towards the planet ring. The fourth moon of the gas giant was habitable, but it was also untouchable.

"We're nearing the danger zone."

"Break off." The Republicans were still heading towards the moon. "The stupid fools."

"Energy spike!"

A beam of energy erupted from one of the countless asteroids that cloaked the moon and made approaching it nearly suicidal. The beam sliced into the frigate and the warship exploded.

"The *Brilliant Moon* has been destroyed."

Vertak nodded. "I can see that for myself." The ship was gone. Not even any significant chunks of debris left to salvage.

"You can hold this system?"

Vertak nodded. "I believe so."

"Be certain, Pack-Master."

"There is only one habitable body in this system and it is untouchable by anyone." He gestured to a display. "The Grah are a world of artists and poets. An agrarian society who live on a garden world with abundant food waiting to picked and a temperate climate." They would be welcome members of the Coalition of Free Systems.

"They have no evidence of technology?"

"None. Their society seems devoid of technology trappings." They wore simple loin clothes and used stone instruments.

"Yet their moon is guarded by an extremely advanced weapon system." Kerloon shrugged. "How do you explain that?"

"Perhaps they used to have advanced technology and decided to return to a simpler lifestyle. Leaving the automated defences to protect them?"

"That is certainly one theory. I've heard another that they all but destroyed themselves in a war and were reduced to that level...leaving the weapons to work without control."

"The level of firepower is considerable."

"We want it."

"So does the Republic."

"But none of us can get it." There were thousands of asteroids orbiting the moon. An unknown percentage contained weapon emplacements. Despite observations, it was impossible to tell which asteroids were merely hunks of rock and which ones contained weaponry...until they fired and no ship had yet survived being fired upon.

"So we skirmish with the Republic. They send ships, we keep ships here, we fight our battles in the emptiness of space."

"Your orders are to watch the system carefully, Pack-Master. See if there is any weakness we can exploit."

"As you wish."

"If possible, we will attempt to land a crew on one of the asteroids."

"A suicide squad?"

"A volunteer squad willing to risk their lives in an attempt to gain new technology. We need some edge if we're to remain free of the Republic's tyranny."

"Shrouding home world with a weapons' array would do it."

Weekend Cruise

"This is not how I envisioned spending our time."

"We are warriors."

"The Duke embraced our willingness to volunteer for the militia...but I doubted he counted on us."

Franz smiled. "Any world can raise some infantry or a tank crew. Even the starfighter pilots have a certain panache." He inhaled the sea breeze. "But a wet navy? Now that is *different*."

"Too different I dare think."

Franz laughed. "Don't worry so much. We're doing our service and still having fun." The Duke had jumped at the offer of several nobles to purchase *military* equipment and fund their own militia unit...no one expected the Jaunty Buccaneers to form a navy.

"We're just a group of young nobles after...what harm can we cause?"

"At least this way we won't get drafted and sent off-world to fight."

* * *

The invasion had proceeded.

"We can't stop them." Duke Karl shook his head grimly. "The Republicans have secured most of the plains around the capitol. The city stands free only because they have not yet chosen to invade it and secure it. I am sure it is only a matter of time now. I can't fight them off."

"Then Meridian is doomed?"

"No...not if we repel the invaders."

"But how can we do that? The bulk of the militia was destroyed in battle."

"I have made arrangements for reinforcements to aid in driving off the Republican fleet. But we must destroy their ground forces."

"How?"

"You are just a group of rabble-rousing, carousing nobles. If you go sailing in your yachts, who will take any notice?" The duke smiled. "And if you sale past the Copper Dam..."

"If the dam breaks, it will flood the plains around the capitol."

"And wash the Republicans away." The Duke nodded with a pleased grin. "The dam is guarded already. Any land-based assault would be doomed to early discovery and failure."

"I understand, my Duke." Franz nodded. He had heard the secret orders in the sharing of idle gossip. "I hear the forecast for tomorrow is rumoured to be clear. A good day for a sail."

* * *

The day was clear and bright.

Franz checked the displays of the Skimmer.

"Looks like a fine day for a cruise."

"I think so." Franz nodded. "The Reps won't know what hit them."

* * *

Franz adjusted the course and speed as the yacht sailed across Obsidian Lake. The dam was a few hundred kilometres ahead.

A *StarHawk* fighter soared past.

Franz waved to it.

"Are you mad?" Ian demanded.

"No...just adding to our cover."

Megan Oberon nodded. "Exactly. We're just a yacht out for a pleasure cruise." The weaponry was hidden from plain sight after all. *No point in advertising our hostile nature to potential foes.*

"We're going to get ourselves killed."

"Not if we're lucky. And if we do get killed, then at least we did our duty."

The trio of yachts accelerated towards the dam.

"Looks like no sign of defenders."

"Oh, there's bound to be some."

As if Franz had conjured them up, two fighters dove from the sky.

"Looks like they've caught on." Megan activated the weaponry. A heavy machine gun rose from behind panels. Megan threw herself into the seat and strapped herself in. She triggered a burst from the guns as the fighters began their strafing run.

"No obvious damage." Franz felt disappointment.

"They'll be coming back around."

"Of course."

The fighters came back, engines screaming.

Megan began hammering at them with all four barrels.

The *Buxom Lass* was struck by missiles and burst into flames.

Franz threw the *Seamist* into an evasive series of twists as laser bolts hissed into the water.

"You're throwing off my aim!" Megan shouted.

"I'm trying to throw off his!" Franz shouted back.

"The dam is getting close."

"Full speed."

"Our missile rack won't be able to breach it."

"Nor will the machine guns." Megan fired another burst and this time scored a hit on one fighter. It pulled up and turned back towards the Republican-held shore.

The other fighter dove again and a laser melted part of the bow.

"Radio report...the Reps have put weapons around the dam. They're gonna be waiting for us."

"Their troops and camps are still downstream, right?"

"So far no sign of evacs."

"Let's hope our spies are accurate." Franz didn't think they were going to make it back alive. "As long as we achieve the mission."

The dam was visible. So were the weapon emplacements.

Missiles streaked towards the two skimmers.

Undertow was hit and lurched.

Franz cursed.

The Republican fighter returned and strafed the stricken skimmer. The crew held their posts and counter fire lanced up at the *StarHawk*. The fighter's right wing was blown off and it slammed into the lake before exploding.

The *Undertow* vanished beneath the waves almost as quickly.

Franz pushed the *Seamist* for all she could give him. The engines were overheating, but it didn't matter.

Defensive fire was blazing around him.

"More speed!" Megan shouted. Moments later, a laser incinerated her machine gun and her.

It didn't matter now.

Franz coughed on smoke. The yacht was burning...but the dam was just ahead. "The Reps won't know what hit them," he muttered.

· *Divided We Will Hang*

"It is the opinion of many that we need to begin coordinating our operations so that we might act in some semblance of unison."

Sky Marshall Eriksson shook his head in careful denial. "I think not, Ambassador McDonnel. The worlds of the Valhalla Sector do not wish to be part of a galaxy-spanning imperium. That is why we chose to secede from the Republic in the first place. For us to now turn and join another multi-world union seems foolish."

The ambassador took a deep breath and gathered his robes of office. "But if all of the Separatist worlds continue to operate separately, then we will eventually be destroyed. The Republic still has considerably more territory and resources than any of us alone can hope to match."

"What do you suggest then?"

McDonnel smiled. *A question I have answered a dozen times already on other worlds.* "A less-binding alliance than the Republic was. No significant ties in politics or merging planetary economies. No, my associates are looking at something far more simply and pragmatic."

"A simple military alliance."

"Precisely, Sky Marshall. If we were to unify our militaries and begin to conduct joint operations—both offensive and defensive—then we stand a far better chance of wearing out the Republic's counterattacks and forcing them to accept our continued independence."

Eriksson quickly shook his head. "Not at this time." He paused to run a hand through his thick reddish beard. "We have a truce of sorts with the local Republican commanders. I will not take any action that might jeopardise that ceasefire."

McDonnel's dark eyes narrowed. "So you will leave the Supremacy and the Grecian League to fight alone?"

"They are looking for war...I only want peace and the right to determine my own course of action. The Republic seems willing to accept that for now."

"Then you are a fool." David McDonnel shook his head. "When the large threats have been destroyed, the Republic *will* come for you...and there will be no one left to protect you."

"I will take that chance. Good day, Ambassador."

* * *

"The *Herald of Change* is prepared for the jump to hyperspace."

"Jump at your discretion then, Captain." McDonnel sighed as he stepped off of the *Comet*-class shuttle. The boxy hanger bay stretched around him, almost empty. "This stop was a waste of time."

The captain offered a polite smile. "Perhaps we will do better at the next world, Ambassador."

McDonnel wearily shook his head. "The Jewel Box is too firmly in the Republican camp," he replied as grey-uniformed technicians brushed past to service the shuttle after its flight. "We will never be able to convince them to secede."

"So why bother going there?"

"Because my brother is serving on one of our frigates—the *Toxic Kiss*—and I want to see him before he departs on the invasion."

"Of course, Ambassador."

"Make the jump, Captain. I have a report to write."

* * *

"I cannot make them understand," Dave said with frustration. "United, we could accomplish much."

"Yet divided we remain."

"The Separatist factions remain separate even from each other. It is so ironic that I feel an urge to scream at each of them in turn." He slumped into the chair and stared at the floor of the officer's quarters. "Instead I am forced to debate their beliefs and argue cold facts."

Commander Conrad McDonnel nodded in agreement. "I often feel that way myself, David."

David looked up at his brother. "But you have a *warship* to back up your requests. I fear that I lack the ability to level a city to express my displeasure."

"Though I am certain you have several targets in mind?"

"Yes." David chuckled ruefully and then reached for the glass of wine he had been ignoring. "I fear it will not aid my cause of unification if I go around destroying major cities amongst those I seek to forge alliances with."

"Not likely."

"It is just so frustrating! The very course of galactic history and civilisation could be forever changed, but no one will listen to me."

"You will continue to travel the space lanes?"

"Of course. I must serve our cause however I can. If that means negotiating with more elected fools, then I will do that."

"What is your overall goal then?"

"A unity of purpose and resources to defeat the Republic. If the various independent states combined their fleets, we could shatter the Republic once and for all."

Conrad frowned. "You are proposing a new offensive?"

"A strike against the capitol." David said that in tones of reverence. "An all-out assault against Metropolis could end the Wars."

Conrad's eyes narrowed as he considered the risks involved...and then the potential gains. "Or plunge the galaxy into even worse conflict."

"You worry too much, Conrad. Without the Senate—"

"Without the Senate, the loyalist worlds could go mad. Without the over-riding guidance from the Admiralty, how would their fleets maintain a firm plan or strategy?"

"They would not...such is my goal. The fleet would be broken into small segments bereft of guidance—and thus easier for us to defeat in detail. The loyalists would turn on each other as new factions seek dominance over the others. It would be chaos and it would be the time for our factions to firmly take hold of the territory we claim."

"And if a certain world decides to launch a bio-chem attack against the League what would stop them?"

The League what would stop them?"

David had no immediate response.

"Or should a group of Senators decide to—"

"I have no time for this. It is all moot speculation anyway because no one wants to listen to my plans."

Conrad smiled. "You have all the answers, don't you?"

"No one listens to me."

"The *Toxic Kiss* will be leaving shortly. We're leading a raid into the Jewel Box. A good strike should disrupt the shipping lanes. Without the exports, local military production should be halved."

David nodded. "That seems like a reasonable assumption. Without a steady supply of focusing crystals, the Republic's shipyards will be unable to arm its new warships."

"This is a good time to strike. We don't know of any significant fleet concentrations in this area. Intelligence has been working overtime to check the sector and I trust the report. The Illustrious Army is spread thin—thinner than their commanders will publicly admit."

David considered the effects of the Republic losing that particular sector. "One good strike and the Jewel Box will fall?"

"Possibly. At the least, the local senator will be screaming for permanent garrison forces."

"If it falls, then we gain a source of focusing crystals and the Republic loses said source." The balance of military power would shift. "If not, the Republic will be forced to divert more units to holding this system...weakening their military efforts elsewhere." A win-win scenario. "Good luck then, Commander." David smiled warmly.

"And where are you heading?"

"Caledonia I think. Another round of debates that will ultimately lead no where."

"Good luck to you then, Ambassador, for I think you will need the luck more than I."

The Suffering Of Innocents

"We consign these resting souls to the embrace of the Mother. She gave you life and now she waits for you still. Sleep easy in her arms."

With a grumbling roar, the bulldozer pushed dirt into the open pit covering the scores of bodies.

"Another nice sermon, Reverend."

"I can do them in my sleep now," he grumbled. Then he yawned. "Is there any word from off-world?" He brushed at grim on his pale tan robes, but was unable to dislodge the dried specks of mud. *Too long*, he thought.

Major Kallenberg shook her head. "None as yet. We remain isolated from the Republic."

"This damned war."

"The sickness seems to have slackened. It's not spreading as fast as it was doing in the storm season."

A feeble light to brighten the gloom of the situation. "We've lost how many hundreds to the plague? How many thousands?"

"A quarter of the population."

"More than that, I think." He looked at the mass grave. "I cannot even tend to each sleeper individually. These mass graves are spreading like the plague."

"You do what you can, Reverend."

"It's not enough." He shook his head. "It's never enough."

"I know." Evandine sighed. "I'm doing all that I can."

"We need outside assistance."

"Which we cannot get. This system is completely isolated."

Reverend Theodore slowly paced towards a tethered mule.

"The fighting has grown out of hand. We are isolated and defeated."

"We never took part in the fighting," he shot back. "We are not a world of warriors. We are simple farmers and miners." He untethered his mule. "What use had we for an interstellar war?" He flicked the reins at her. "Most of us do not even have working vehicles any longer."

She made no reply but grimly took the reins of her own mule. The bulldozer that was covering the grave was a military vehicle.

"What use do the combatants have for us?" The more telling question. "We are of no use to the Republic nor the Separatists. Once they isolated us, both sides promptly lost interest."

"I'm confidant the communications will be restored soon."

"We're under a blockade aren't we?"

"The last I heard we were. The Consortium, I think."

"And for what? Just to see how long it will take us to die?"

"I don't know what they want."

"Us dead. Our world for their war games. Our mules." Theodore snorted and the mule echoed him. "We are lost."

"The people still respect you."

"I have given them guidance...while the military governor says little."

"My ability is limited. God, Theodore, I was a Captain five months ago. Before the plague."

"The Gods have deserted us I fear. They chastise us with this sickness as a punishment for our sins."

"I'm not so certain that this is an act of your gods. It's too virulent, too sudden."

"You hold to the theory that the Separatists unleashed this sickness upon us as a weapon?"

"They've been using biochemical attacks for the last year. Perhaps we were a test world for a new strain."

"A fitting punishment."

"We need to regain contact with Metropolis."

"I cannot commune across light-years. Your technical problems are your own."

"I need parts and some of the Frenzied River tribe have a cache I need to examine."

"The tribes have little use for shiny metal."

"They occupy a supply cache the Republic set up centuries ago. I need to see it."

"They refuse you access?"

"Yes. They would not refuse *you*."

"I take no sides in your disputes with the natives of this world. I merely teach them spiritual guidance."

"The Republic could cure the plague. We have doctors and medicines. We can help...if we can contact them."

"I will speak with the tribe elders...assuming any still breath."

"Thank you, Theodore."

Dining On Ashes

Don Williams ducked behind a pockmarked brick wall as a *Typhoon*-class hovertank rumbled down the street. Its turret was topped by what looked to be a pulse laser. "Scavengers," he muttered. The wind howled mournfully around the ruined buildings of the former office blocks. The capitol was a wasteland now.

* * *

"The city is almost deserted. It's been picked over pretty clear already."

"Gather what you can, then we'll head out." Jeff Morgan looked around with a grim frown. "This place is dead." The wind was whistling mournfully through the ruined buildings and it sounded like the wailing of lost souls. "How did things come to this?" he asked.

"Looks like the Charnox got here first."

"The local defenders probably never even knew what hit them then."

"Not likely, Sir."

The hovertank shifted its turret in a slow sweep of the horizon. No sign of ambushers, but its crew were taking no chances. Armoured troopers stood ready for action, but most seemed resigned rather than tense.

Jeff frowned. "Survivors?" he asked. He sipped tepid water from his canteen and sighed. *I need something stronger..*

"No sign of any yet. Either they've left the capitol...." The scout didn't bother to finish his statement.

Jeff shook his head. "Too late," he muttered. "All right," a touch of military crispness filled his voice. "I want you to divide into squads and spread out. Sweep this area for survivors and any supplies we can carry. We'll need all the supplies we can gather if we're going to continue the fight."

"The fight is over," a trooper muttered. "We got pounded."

"The fight is not over!" Jeff snapped. "We are Republican soldiers. We will continue to act as such. If the rest of the Republic falls, then at least *we* will remain loyal to its ideals!"

A small clatter of falling bricks caused the troopers to whirl around and aim their weapons towards the noise.

"Come out with your hands raised!" Jeff called in basic. "Or else."

"I'm coming out!" a Human voice called back. A feminine voice.

The woman was ragged and filthy. Her hair was matted and greasy, and her clothes were more rags than jumpsuit. "Thank heavens. You're Republicans?"

"Jeff Morgan, Captain of the Ninety-Second Dragoons."

"Carol Hartford. Poet." She laughed nervously. "A useless occupation during a war."

Jeff watched his squad turn back to their examination of the ruins. "You lived here?" he asked in a softer voice.

Carol nodded. "I was one of the locals. Before we got flattened."

"Who attacked you?"

She shrugged. "No idea. If they named themselves first, I never found out. The first I heard about the invasion was when the ChatterNet went down."

"Sounds like the Slinks," an armoured trooper suggested. "They usually take out a planet's satellites and communications first...then they hit the capitol with an orbital bombardment to crush resistance before it can start. It looks like that is what happened here."

"But why us?" Carol demanded. "What did we do to them?"

"Nothing." Jeff shrugged. "We just left ourselves vulnerable to them."

"I thought the Wars were on the other side of the galaxy."

"They are...for the most part."

* * *

The column of armoured trucks and tanks rumbled back towards the deserted spaceport.

"This is the face of civilisation." Jeff gestured to the abandoned ruins as his convoy made its slow way towards the outskirts of the city. "Humanity is facing extinction. It's the collapse of civilisation as we know it."

"How did it come to this?" Carol shook her head. She was riding in one of the trucks, beside the captain. *The only civilian survivor,* she thought numbly. *I can't be...there have to be others.* But the Republicans lacked the time or personnel to make a long search. *They must be hiding outside the capitol...in the farming communities. Assuming any of them are still standing.* "The Republic was at peace. We were expanding throughout the stars. We were colonizing planet after planet. The whole galaxy was at peace."

"We lived with the illusion of peace, but it was the peace of the gun." Jeff failed to keep the bitterness from his voice. *Hindsight is always twenty/twenty,* he thought grimly. "The Republic maintained order throughout the territory it had claimed through the Judicial Forces and their quasi-military muscle. It worked for a quite long time, as long as the bulk of member worlds allowed the system to work. With the Separatists suddenly splitting off and taking their manpower and military equipment with them, it left the system weakened. Fatally."

"But President Tiresias—"

"Is one man. He tried to maintain order, but the Separatists wanted war."

"And they got it. Half the galaxy is in flames right now. Or so the ChatterWeb said."

"It's fairly accurate. Dozens of small political unions have sprung up, all diverting resources from the loyalist systems. The Republic was at peace, but our neighbours weren't."

"The Hyderabad Sector was always peaceful."

"You were too small to be otherwise." Jeff laughed bitterly. "This sector is an afterthought really. There is only one safe route through local hyperspace to connect you with the rest of the Republic. Your sector exports almost nothing to the core worlds and you import even less. Even before the war, this sector operated pretty much as an autonomous region. You barely got taxed...not worth the effort to send ships to collect the trade tariffs."

"We are loyal to the Republic. We have done nothing to support the Separatists."

"True, but how much of that stems from a lack of military resources?" Jeff laughed again at her outrage. "My Dragoons are the most powerful military unit in the region. We could have seized the sector easily."

"You could," Carol agreed, "and you would be welcomed by most of the people. With the wars raging, people crave safety."

"One lure of the Separatists' banner. 'We're closer than Metropolis so we can protect you better from whatever enemies you think that you have.' Imagined enemies become real...and so you and your new allies to go to war."

"We were at war with no one."

"You were of no worth to anyone." Jeff laughed bitterly. "One key problem with this sector is that the Human worlds are few and resource poor. Your neighbours have all the power."

Carol nodded. "We seldom had contact with either of them. I preferred the Slinks to the Charnox though."

Jeff frowned. "Those two species were another hindrance of Republic expansion in this region." The reptilian Slinks and the canine Charnox were the dominate native lifeforms and both had colonized several dozen worlds throughout the area. Humans had only been able to claim resource-poor and otherwise worthless planets. "We should have seen this coming."

"We had no idea. We thought the raids were minor things." Carol shrugged. "They raided each other almost constantly."

"The Judicial Forces kept a lid on the worst of it." Three divisions had been stationed in this sector before the Secession Wars erupted. "Unfortunately, once the bulk of our units were withdrawn and sent off to the distant warfronts, the Slink and Charnox went to war with a passion...and neither side was too picky about choosing their potential battlefields or respecting the boundaries of other races."

Carol took a breath. "What are the other sector worlds like?"

"About the same."

Carol's face paled. "How widespread have the attacks been?" she asked in a tense voice. "The entire Republic can't have been hit."

"It's not. But the hyperspace route has been cut off. Too much fighting in the Sambalpur System...every ship trying to jump has been attacked and destroyed or captured. One or two traders might have jumped successfully, but no one has come back from Metropolis." Most likely, the Senate had written off the entire sector as a waste of resources desperately required elsewhere. "As for the rest of Hyderabad..." He paused, gathering his thoughts. "There might be a few worlds still intact, but I haven't heard of any. The Star-Net is down. Most of the sector's worlds are isolated now. Easy pickings for the scavengers."

"And you're one of them?"

"It's the only way to live now."

"It's horrible."

"If you makes you feel any better, the Slinks and Charnox are no better off. Between their own war, plus Dragoon-led reprisals, most of their worlds have been reduced to smouldering rubble." A touch of pride coloured his words. "They are no longer a serious threat." It had been costly, launching those counterassaults, but necessary. *No one can attack our worlds with impunity. It will take them centuries to rebuild their infrastructure.* It would probably take centuries for the Humans to do likewise, of course, without the rest of the Republic to call upon.

"It doesn't matter. We should be above this." Carol gestured to the tanks and soldiers. "We should be at peace, not waging a war."

"The war is over, lady." He shook his head. "We had lost it before we even knew we under attack." The spaceport came into sight. Blocky shuttles waiting on their pads, behind a ring of armed guards.

* * *

The *Vainglorious* broke orbit.

"How long until we jump?"

"An hour or so at current burn. We're taking time accelerating to jump-ready speed." Conserving fuel until they could restock.

"Good enough then."

"What's our next target?"

"Meridian was a waste of time. I say we head for Meadowvale."

"I'll plot a suitable course."

* * *

Carol stared at the star map. "I can't believe that it's all gone," she said. *So many worlds. So many people.*

"The attackers were fierce. A defended world might fight off the first attack...and the second. But they just kept coming. Eventually, even the strongest world was worn down and its defences broken."

"So there is no hope for us?"

"For us in particular? Or for the Republic? Or for our race in general?"

"Any of them. All of them."

Jeff smiled. "There is always hope."

* * *

Ryan stared into the candle's flame. It was hypnotic, addictive. So easy to lose one's self in the flickering glow for hours on end.

He shook his head to clear it. "I saw a fish." A fish whose scales were quickly lost amongst the stars. He blew the candle out. "I see our course. I must walk that path." He reached for the intercom. "Set a course for Aquaris."

"Yes, Sir."

* * *

"Aquaris orbit ahead, Captain."

Ryan stood watching from an unoccupied bridge station.

"We'll restock the tanks with fresh water." Starships always needed new supplies of potable water for the crew's drinking and bathing, as well as to supply hydrogen for the fusion reactors. "Set a course for orbit. Hail the planet on normal frequencies. Maybe one or two of the cities are still down there."

"Yes, Captain."

"Jeff, prepare your troops for a mission."

"Defend the shuttles?"

"Hopefully you won't encounter resistance."

"Hopefully, Captain, we'll find survivors."

New Reef was mostly submerged, but a portion of the city still floated above the waves.

Carol looked around. "It's awful."

"It used to be a nice city. Now there is only this." A few square blocks at most. Jeff shook his head. "It looks like an aerial assault hit the place hard. Broke the flotation blocks and caused most of this place to go straight to the ocean's bottom."

"Great."

"The entire planet is ocean." A storm was brewing, he could feel it in the wind. "I doubt we'll find any survivors here." Not unless they were half-fish. *Probably a Slink attack...the Charnox hate water.*

"The barges are filling their tanks."

"We'll launch as soon as the *Vainglorious's* tanks are full."

"That might take several trips."

"I know, but we can't keep travelling with our reserves almost gone. We'll stay in orbit for as long as necessary." The system seemed safe enough. "Have the barges launch when full, transfer their cargo to the *Vainglorious*, and then return here for another load."

"Yes, Commander."

"Then we'll head for another world."

"And see more devastation?" Carol asked.

"There might be survivors on the next world we visit. We might even find a world untouched by the invasion."

"Do you really believe that?"

"I try to believe it. If this," he gestured to the wreckage, "is all that remains of the Republic, then why should we try to go on living?"

* * *

"Vessels on scope!"

"Identify them."

"Looks like a pack of Charnox."

"Damn." Captain Kimball-Holland cursed and then cleared his throat.

"What are we going to do?"

"We have generally have two choices to us: run or fight."

"We're going to fight?" Jeff asked.

"No, we're going to run. I don't want to tangle with that much firepower. Full power to the drives. Get us to the jump-point. Fast."

"Aye, Captain."

"No point in fighting," Ryan commented from the comm-station. "We have nothing here to defend." The Charnox could not strip-mine a water world of all of its resources.

* * *

"Welcome to Bombay."

She stared at the monitor. "Those look like asteroids."

"They are. A dozen asteroids were towed here from the asteroid belt and then hollowed out and armed with surface batteries. The Republic wanted to make sure that this particular world was defended from pirates." The Charnox had been envious of Bombay's mineral wealth for decades. "So far, they've managed to hold back pirates, raiders, and outright assaults."

"So one world still has the Republic's glory?"

"Yeah." *For now.* "I told you that I had hope for something beyond the collapse of the Republic."

"I should have listened."

The orbital defences were impressive for a former provincial world. Half a dozen space stations were in orbit above the planet, and scores of weapon-laden platforms accompanied them.

"It looks secure."

"It should. I hate to think how much of the planetary income is being spent on upgrading weaponry."

"Not quite the level of Metropolis."

"No, we don't have their level of SpaceGuard stations, but we're secure enough here for now."

"Bombay is the acting capitol of the Bombay Alliance."

"You're not rebuilding the Republic Sector Government?"

"The Republic failed us." Governor-Elect Francesca Kimball-Holland offered a shrug, then hastily adjusted her shawl. "Why would we want to recreate the failures of the past? This Alliance is the best way to lead the surviving pockets of Humanity into the future."

"A few systems worlds so far, but we're adding more," Captain Peter Kimball-Holland added with a smile. "It's slow work though."

"I thought the other worlds were destroyed?"

"We're rebuilding."

"I see." Carol frowned. "Jeff never mentioned this."

"Jeff remains loyal to the ideals of the Republic. The path that we are taking the Human citizens down is not one that he can feel comfortable following. So he prefers to dream that the Republic will be reborn."

"Won't that happen?"

"We're cut off from Metropolis," the Governor replied. "We have no support from the Illustrious Army. We have no major battle fleets, not even a trading fleet worth attracting pirates. Despite my cousin's beliefs and exploits, we have no major space capability. The Dragoons have shattered the Charnox and the Slink so we are relatively safe to rebuild. But I will not wait patiently for the Senate to send us aid."

"But you are rebuilding?"

"Not every world was shattered beyond repair, Carol. In most cases, the worlds around this sector were poor and lacking useful resources for the Charnox or Slink to take. They hit the military or industrial targets and then turned and ran, leaving us to rebuild. Only major worlds were flattened, and most of the initial attacks were actually launched by accident."

"Accident," Carol repeated. "We were destroyed by accident?"

"Yes, an accident. Each side feared that we would side with the other so each launched a series of raids to distract us. The raids proved bloodier than any of us anticipated."

"Our counter-attack proved bloodier than they expected as well," Jeff said as he stepped into the office. He was wearing a fresh uniform. "The arrival of the *Vainglorious* above the Charnox's main shipyards was most unexpected." He smiled wolfishly. "A few volleys of turbolasers into their reactor cores and the Charnox won't be expanding their military forces any time soon."

"And you gave a similar treatment to the Slinks?"

"Yes, but the *Ironheart* failed to survive its attack." Peter made that comment in a quiet voice. The sacrifice of the frigate had eliminated the Slink threat though...no one wanted to contemplate the effects of a crippled frigate falling out of orbit and slamming into the capital city.

Carol shook her head again. "We're on what was considered the far side of the Republic. The bulk of the current battlefields are far away, so we were not hit all that hard."

"Hard enough," Jeff said.

"True."

"We lost five worlds to nuclear attacks. Those worlds will not be rebuilt."

"I did not mean to discount those losses."

"Good."

"It just seems like a waste."

"It was. Any war is a waste, Carol. All we can do is rebuild and hope that we are not attacked again."

"What do you want me to do?"

"You are a poet. You have a talent for using words, right?"

"Yes."

"I would like you to join my entourage as a morale officer of sorts. Help write speeches and poems to inspire the citizens of the Alliance to new heights of greatness."

"And if I cannot?"

"Then we will continue on...without the illusion of hope."

"Hope is no illusion," Jeff told her. "Remember how you felt on Jakarata when we found you in the ruins? You were desperate to hear that the Republic still stood...we have millions of people who feel the same desperation. Won't you do what you can to help them?"

One Big Basket

"Welcome to the Fokkers-Mitsubishi Starplex, Ambassador."

"Thank you, Star Admiral." The Human smiled warmly.

Star Admiral Chorfa-nak raised his crest slightly. "The battle was fiercely fought. Much honour was gained and lost in this campaign."

"You have captured the most important shipyard in the galaxy...an achievement your hatchlings will cherish for generations."

"I wish the cost had not been so high." Chorfa-nak clicked his beak.

"You have wounded the Republic...a blow from which they will not readily recover."

Chorfa-nak eyed the Human. "It cost us many ships."

"It cost the Republic many more. It also cost them the chance to repair their damaged ones, or build new ones." David McDonnel smiled happily. "This is an important day for us." He glanced through the view ports of the *Dark Majesty's* bridge at the scene beyond. Space stations, shipyards of varying sizes, and scores and scores of warships. "It was a battle worthy of legend."

"A surprise attack gained us little honour."

"A frontal attack would have cost you even more heavily."

"The garrison units are already being assigned to hold this system. The rest of the Wing will be ready to deploy to other sectors as needed. The Wars will continue."

"You are ordered to stand on the defensive for now. The Provisional Council has decided to make holding this system a priority. The Republic cannot allow us to hold it...they will launch a counterattack. You are to bleed them. Weaken their fleets until they can no longer muster strength enough to attack."

"Weaken them until they bargain for peace?"

"Precisely."

"I see."

"The garrison fleet is large enough for you?"

"It rivals that of many sector capitols." The Star Admiral gestured to one of the bridge displays. "Twenty frigates and forty corvettes. Plus another thirty or so converted freighters being used as troop transports."

"Will four divisions be enough marines?"

"I do not know." The Starplex was heavily populated.

"You have many PreyDroids."

"I know. I will need them to hold this system."

"You have done well, Star Admiral. This is a great day for the Separatist Cause."

* * *

"The loss of the Starplex is a dark one." President Tiresias stood in his office and stared through the armoured windows at the cityscape. "Our offensive operations will be crippled."

"Damaged ships will be difficult to repair without those yards. The military forces of a dozen sectors relied on those yards to keep their vessels operational. The loss is a dear one."

"The Separatists knew exactly where to hit us."

"It cost them, President."

"Do you have casualty numbers?"

"Nothing confirmed."

"Estimates then?"

"Ten frigates and seventeen corvettes lost by the Separatists, a few hundred PreyDroid fighters. The defending units suffered heavy losses before withdrawing. Two dreadnoughts, thirty cruisers, twenty-four corvettes. No firm numbers on *StarHawks* yet, but a few hundred easily."

Tiresias winced.

"Civilian losses are unknown. The Separatists used converted freighters as fighter carriers and troop transports. A lot of confusion resulted when the first PreyDroids launched…the civilians freighters were victims of considerable friendly fire."

"I cannot fault Admiral Stewart for that decision. Holding the yards was a priority."

"The Admiral died with her flagship. It did destroy several enemy units during the second wave. With her death, the defence collapsed and the remaining units jumped to Farsund to regroup."

"We must retake the yards." And quickly too.

"I will assign Admiral Takeda to retake the Starplex. He is one of our finest officers."

"Do what you must. Requisition whatever resources you deem necessary. The recapture of those shipyards are now deemed a priority mission."

"Yes, Mister President."

"Without too much damage if possible?"

"Of course. Reports indicate that the Zorya and Oro Yards took some damage."

"I see."

"They were the older lines, President, and were not at full production in any event. Admiral Stewart focused on defending the Asshur and Ares Yards. Our military strength should not suffer lasting harm."

"If the Starplex is retaken."

"True."

Strength Of The Past

"We've got power." The lights were dim, but growing in intensity. "The reactor is back online. Safety protocols are all showing green." Phaedra tapped at the control panel with her delicate fingers. "I think we've got a chance."

"You're kidding me, right?"

"I've never been more serious."

"You've never been more insane! The Gronop are raiding throughout this sector and you're looking at museum pieces."

"We need to defend ourselves."

"This *Cavalier*-class frigate hasn't been operational in centuries."

"I know. I think we can get it running again."

"We're going to get killed."

"You worry too much, Declan." Phaedra smiled as she checked the console again. "We can do this you know."

* * *

The small fleet of frigates broke orbit and accelerated towards the separatist task force.

"Incoming warships."

Loren Turner laughed loudly as the report from his aide arrived. "Look at them!" he scoffed. "A hundred metres long, if that. Museum pieces. One hit from our weapons and they will crumble." He laughed more loudly. "An easy mission we got assigned. A cake-walk."

* * *

"Open fire!" Phaedra ordered. The bright lasers stabbed from their cannons. Four lasers per ship splashing from the deflector screens of the lead brigantine.

"There's only three enemy ships."

"We have them outnumbered then, Declan."

He shook his head. "Just one of those ships has us out-gunned," he reminded his commander. "They're bigger than we are too."

"And more heavily armed," Phaedra added with a dry smile.

"We can't win."

"We have no choice! We can't leave Mica Major undefended. Every single crewmember has volunteered to fight to defend our world and these *museum* pieces are all that we have available."

Declan sighed again. "I know...I volunteered too."

"You always had a soft spot for me." Phaedra paused to pull at the braids holding her brown hair in an intricate coil. "Let's get 'em!"

"Our deflectors are holding."

Loren Turner was amazed by the need of his tactical officer to make the comment. "Of course they are. Those lasers can't harm the *Blood in the Water*." What could those Mica Majority fools hope to accomplish? "Target one of them and open fire. Demonstrate our firepower."

"Energy spike!"

A barrage of turbolasers converged on one of the Cavaliers and blew the small frigate into molten scarp.

"Ye Gods!" Phaedra swore.

"Damn!" Declan added. "We're seriously outgunned, Commander."

"*Rabid Leer* has been destroyed. No lifepods."

"All ships, concentrate fire on the killer. Stand by to fire missiles on my mark." She grimaced. "Fire lasers!"

"What do they think they're doing?"

"Those lasers are straining the screens, Captain!"

"Impossible!"

"Impossible for one ship...the whole fleet is combining fire on us. Our screens can't absorb that level of energy for long."

Loren chewed at his lip for a moment. "Target them and open fire. Scatter them."

"Deflector screen is failing!"

"Get the back-up systems on-line!"

"I'm trying."

"They've launched missiles!"

"Brace for impact!" Loren shouted.

The *Blood In The Water* shuddered.

"Hull breaches in the forward sections."

"Casualty reports coming in."

Loren winced as he picked himself off the deck. "This was supposed to be an easy mission...it seems to be growing more difficult." He could feel bruises forming on his legs and chest.

"Your orders?"

"We're still operational?"

"Yes, Captain."

"Status of the enemy fleet?"

"Two ships destroyed, three damaged. All the others are turning around for another attack run."

"Fend them off. Fire at will! Get those screens restored."

"Yes, Captain."

"We hurt him, by God!" Phaedra allowed her voice to broadcast her pleasure at that report.

"He hurt us back."

"I know." Phaedra's tone turned sullen. "It is going badly."

"We need reinforcements."

"We need a miracle."

"Still no response from Typhoon's Cove Anchorage."

"The loyalists are still scattered. We're on our own." Surrounded by separatist worlds and hostile systems. "I hope we can hold out."

* * *

Two hours' delayed in this little skirmish...I would not have thought it possible! Grimly squashing that mental voice, Loren studied the still-functioning displays. "*Deadly Reign* is still fully operational?"

"Yes, Captain."

"Order it to break formation and head towards the planet."

"Aye, Captain."

"Orbital strike at Gregory's discretion."

"Prepare to take us in for another attack run."

"Copy that, Captain."

"I'm sure we can make more runs." Declan held up a small pad. "We're hurting badly. *Heart of the Wolf* and *Ladies of the Tower* are both derelicts—I doubt either ship has a working weapon or thruster."

"We've battered *Blood* and hurt that other ship."

"So *Dark Lord's Wrath* is drifting too...big deal. Either of those other two battleships is still more than enough to finish us off. Us and *Dreamwalker* and *Weaving Wheel*."

"Phaedra, *Deadly Reign* has broken formation. It's accelerating towards Mica."

"Show me."

"We can't stop it. We're barely holding the others in check."

"We can't let that monster reach Mica."

"Take us about, full power to remaining weapons."

"*Blood* is moving to intercept us."

"*Dreamwalker* is accelerating! Closing on *Reign*."

"Good luck, Mitchell," Phaedra said in a soft voice. "Fire missiles at the other ships! Distract them before they can assist their ally."

"Copy that!"

"Point defence is engaging the missiles...I don't expect any to penetrate."

"Keep the screens braced for impacts."

"*Dreamwalker* is on a collision course with *Reign*!"

"Tell Gregory is evade!"

"No response...we're being jammed."

"Damn it! This cannot be happening. Those are old museum relics! We have top-of-the-line warships!" Loren winced as the battered frigate, its hull alight with explosions from the *Reign's* guns, collided with the larger ship and both vessels were consumed in a fireball.

"No lifepods detected."

"Stand by to head for Mica. We're going to level that mud ball."

"Captain?"

"Our orders no longer matter. Mica has cost us too much to recover by conquest. Now we'll destroy it."

"Captain, distress signal from *Dark Lord*—it's been rammed!"

"What?" Loren screamed. "How?"

"While we were distracted by the *Dreamwalker*, *Heart of the Wolf* suddenly fired its thrusters and rammed. *Dark Lord* has lost power. Its reactor is shutting down."

"Tactical, defensive fire on batteries!" A note of urgency coloured his voice. "I don't want any of those other ships to slip past our defences." He was eyeing the remaining frigates with healthy and newfound fear. "Move us towards the *Dark Lord* and stand by to recover its crew."

"Yes, Captain."

"They're moving off."

"We've won then." Phaedra smiled. "Victory!"

"At a cost," Declan added.

"There's always a cost," she agreed, "but this time we've won the safety of our home world by paying it."

"I just hope it was really worth all the blood and lives this skirmish cost." Declan slumped into his chair. "We can't afford to fight another battle."

"I know." Phaedra's coiled hair was a mess. "Alert the recovery crews to assist *Ladies*. We'll watch our guests until they withdraw."

"You don't think they'll press their attack."

"Not now that they've seen how desperate we are. Our lasers can't hurt their ships...but ramming attacks can. And ramming is about all these relics can do now."

Shadow Dagger

"Take cover!"

"Security?"

"Well they're not techs."

"Just what we need." Miguel ducked behind a crate. "How are we supposed to finish this job?"

"Keep working." Patrick checked his portable scanner. "Looks like just one squad."

"Eight troopers too many."

"I can take them out. Just keep working." He hurried away from the parked tank and hurried towards the vehicle park's outer wall. He quickly checked his technician's uniform for obvious flaws, then turned his attention to the computer scanner in his left hand.

The door hissed open.

Three figures entered. Their gender and species was obscured by the body armor each wore. They carried rifles in their hands.

"Who're you?" one demanded.

"Damian Stevens, Technician Level-Two."

"Identification?"

He handed over a data card. "I've got to get the tanks checked over. The Commander'll have my head otherwise."

"Get to it, Tech." The trooper gestured. "I have no time to waste on you." He gave the array of tanks a quick glance over through his visor. "The rebels are gathering outside the city. Those *Marksmen* are going to be needed to crush those scum."

"They'll be ready for the battle."

Patrick watched the troopers leave. "Those aren't elites," he scoffed. "Barely adequate for regular militia."

Miguel climbed out of one of the *Marksmen*. "I've got this one checked out." He smiled. "All systems will show combat-ready...until they actually reach the battlefield."

"We'll need to hurry. The attack could start any moment...and we won't want to get caught here when it does."

"Then get helping me." Miguel popped the hatch on another tank. "The faster we finish, the sooner we can get out of here."

* * *

"The battle of Korinda was short."

Patrick nodded to his superior. "The assault began on schedule and the defenders moved out of their base precisely as planned. They moved towards the Plains of Tarkis along the main highway Once they reached the Bridge of Lotus Blossoms, the first elements of the Grim Determination hit their flanks."

"And your sabotage efforts took effect."

"Seven of the twelve tanks shut down as programmed." Miguel and himself had entered a computer virus into the tank's computer system during their infiltration. "The other five *Marksmen* were disabled in battle."

"Losing the bridge cost them the battle. We were able to push across to the Plains and reach the city before it could be reinforced."

"Lieutenant Saunders captured the government offices before the governor could be evacuated."

"The fact that we had air supremacy helped in that regard." Colonel Tyler checked the data pad he was holding. "Your strike team is receiving a commendation, of course, for their efforts."

"All part of our job," Patrick replied. "We are officers of the H.S.B."

"The Hegemony Security Bureau has certain standards to maintain. So far we have never failed in any operation assigned to us by the Archon. The failure of the former Republican Security Bureau led to the start of the Secession Wars. I will not allow this department to suffer a similar lapse in its observations."

"Have you new assignment for me?"

"You're still on leave, Captain." Tyler smiled. "I'm certain you will be called upon soon enough. There're still hundreds of hot spots in the galaxy requiring Intelligence to intervene."

* * *

The corridors of the intelligence outpost were quiet.

Patrick glanced over his shoulder as he moved through one corridor junction. Although there were half a dozen people present, almost none of them were talking.

Patrick stopped outside one door. He typed his code into the keypad. The door hissed open.

"Captain."

"Doctor Dorvan." He nodded to the scientist. "How goes it?"

"The infernal thing is keeping its secrets." Dorvan gestured to the metallic box with a grunt. "Almost three months and I still know little more than how to turn it on." His glare spoke eloquently. "I believe the machine is a data storage device, but I'm not certain."

"You're supposed to be one of the best minds we have. How can you be stumped?"

"It's an alien device." Dorvan shrugged. "And I mean *alien*. The dig was on a planet abandoned for centuries. Possibly longer."

"Surely it can't be that difficult to check."

"Some of the technology in use inside this box is beyond current Hegemony abilities." He shook his head in disbelief. "There is a lot of gel-type circuitry...almost as if this was a *living* machine." He laughed. "An absurd thought, is it not?"

"Organic tech? That's not totally beyond belief, Doctor."

"It is beyond my abilities to study. I work with computer technology. I can decipher programming datatracks. This bio-tech is new to me."

"I can call in other scientists." The H.S.B. had placed this project under some priority.

"That would be helpful. Some of the operatives in this facility are less than helpful to my requests."

"They don't know you."

"If I didn't know better, I would suspect some of them as plotting against the H.S.B."

Patrick shook his head. "Impossible. The staff here have all been vetted by L.O." The Loyalty Operatives were relentless in their quest to root out potential traitors before they could act; for a brief moment, Patrick wondered if Dorvan could be a member of the L.O.—no one knew the true identities of those operatives.

"L.O. has been mistaken before."

"The Archon has implemented new agents to oversee the safety of his security bureau."

"I wonder what level of security this device has." The scientist was eyeing the alien computer again. "Perhaps if I tried a new series of algorithms, I could crack the encoding."

"I'll leave you to your work then."

Patrick stepped into the corridor. It was still deserted. "I hope I get another mission soon," he muttered aloud. "Too long in this place will drive me insane." The quiet was getting to him.

Profit Sharing

"Important, this shipyard remains."

"Not as important as Fokkers-Mitsubishi though."

"No, but we are still a system courted by the Republic and by two different separatist factions."

"That leaves us a profit to reap."

"Hopefully a good one."

"Any profit a good one is."

The Arkanites chuckled.

One of the non-Arkanites grumbled something.

"A comment you have, Krun?"

Looking up from a pile of hardcopy notes, the Security Director nodded. "Yes, Station Director. We remain vulnerable during the chaos of war."

"Good for business this war is."

"But harmful to commerce. Pirate attacks are increasing daily."

"Deal with them you must."

"I do what I can with limited resources," Krun told them. "Control of a shipyard is vital for any faction hoping to win the ongoing war. You have all seen the reports of fighting over the Fokkers-Mitsubishi Yards. The Separatists took considerable casualties when they moved to secure that facility for their own use...the Hegemony's counterattack was equally fierce." It would take months for both sides to repair damaged warships and probably years to replace the hulls lost in both of those fierce battles. "A nominally independent system like ours will be a beacon to those desperate to seize a source of new ships."

"Treaties we have."

"Defences we have."

"Attack us no one will. Secure we remain."

"Playing all factions off each other will work for a time, but sooner or later one side will attempt to move in and take over the entire system. We must increase our local defences."

"Increase our defences?" The Station Director set the hardcopy he was holding down onto the granite tabletop. He blinked his eyes several times.

"Protect ourselves we must. Vulnerable, our assets are."

"A waste of money."

Krun grunted. "Commerce raiders have been attacking freighters near the asteroid mines."

"Pirate scum."

"Nonetheless, Director, these raids are disrupting the flow of resources to the Yards. We cannot afford to lose too many shipments or our production rates will falter."

"Our profits that would cut."

"Indeed."

"Increase patrols you must."

The Haung shrugged its massive shoulders. "I do what I can with the assets available to me, but our system patrollers are limited in number." Ironic that a system dominated by a massive shipyard facility should possess an insufficient number of patrol craft with which to defend itself.

"Dissent on Chammandar is slowing the delivery of the Desrick Mark VIII nav-computers."

"Delay production that will."

"We cannot complete starships without functional computer cores. As well to build them without working hyperdrives."

"Send ships to *encourage* our suppliers you must."

Divide my already weak defence assets? "Find another supplier. Make the Chammandar fear to lose our business." The Gold Star'arx Shipyards were the largest consumers of Desrick computers in the galaxy…losing that business could bankrupt the entire Chammandar home world.

"Profit before all else?"

"Aye."

"More sniper raids on our shipping. Disruptions are continuing."

"Unacceptable this is."

"I can nothing about it. I need more patrol ships. Divert one of the lesser yards to produce a few squadrons of pinnances for me and I will be able to increase my patrols."

"Unnecessary this expense is."

"A minor expense."

"Hrmph."

"I have sent the blueprints to the Yards. No hyperdrives, no navigation computer. No hanger bays. Just a cockpit on a fuselage with an array of laser cannon." *Not even the fancier turbolasers, just basic lasers. No missiles to restock after a battle either.*

"An oversize fighter this is."

"Basically. Just enough life support ability to patrol the system for a few weeks before returning to port. A small crew so it's more economical to operate. Basically it's meant to escort freighters along the mining routes."

"Consider this I will."

"Thank you, Director."

"New business we have coming." The Director bared his teeth. "No trouble! No pirates. No sabotage. Disturb our guests, nothing must!"

Krun nodded. "System Security will be deployed in force."

"Raiders incoming!"

"Demonspawn!" Krun snarled. "Lasers fire at will." He swung his small pinnance around and accelerated towards the pirate. His gunners fired a barrage from the forward laser battery and the beams splattered against the raider's screens. *I needed to get away from the Directors' Board,* he thought with a wry smile. *But this is a little more action than I had counted on though.* A good field test of the small escort ships he had finally managed to have had built.

Return fire scorched hull plating.

"We're outnumbered."

"Order the convoy to scatter. Maybe some of them can escape." There were a lot of pirates in the area though—at least five corvette-sized vessels with thirty fighters.

Ships reverted from hyperspace. Angular vessels bristling with firepower and broadcasting Hegemony transponder beacons.

"*Peremptory* to pirate vessels. Stand down or be destroyed."

"They're firing!"

Krun smiled. "Fools."

"Thank you for your aid, we do, Captain Crukshank."

The blond Human stood tall and proud in his black uniform. "This system and its shipyards are vital to our continued survival and our eventual victory," he said to the beings seated around the conference room. "As of this moment, the Gold Star'arx Yards are being placed under Hegemony control."

The Director blinked several times.

"Protest we do!" one of the other Arkanites exclaimed.

"Independent we are."

"The Archon has requested that all essential systems be placed under direct military control for the duration of the current crisis. The Senate has seconded the motion."

"Conquered we are?"

"Protected by a loyal Hegemony garrison. You are harassed by raiders, as I observed upon my arrival." He smiled at the memory of how quickly the pirates had been vaporised by his warships' raw firepower.

"Contracts with many worlds we have."

"You are a loyal member of the Hegemony, are you not?" the officer asked with a sly grin. He looked around the conference room. The natives were barely half his size, and he knew they had already seen the garrisons of body-armoured troopers moving through the corridors of Arkhold Station.

"Signed the Republic Charter we did. The Hegemony, Captain, we know not."

"The Republic is gone!" the Human said. "The Celestial Hegemony has risen from the ashes to replace it. You will assist in the defeat of the Separatist traitors." His voice hardened. "Or else you will be considered to be in league with them."

"And occupied?" Krun asked grimly.

Crukshank looked at the Haung with a small smile. "The Archon will not allow the member worlds of the Hegemony to be threatened by any other power. Shipyards supplying hostile fleets would certainly have to be *neutralised*." He smiled after delivering the veiled threat. "You do understand the reasoning for this, of course?"

For The Grace Of God

"We have entered orbit, Deacon-Prince."

Dormus nodded once as he surveyed the command deck. His crew-males laboured at their stations without haste or unseemly noise. "Any response from the infidels?" he asked in a loud voice. *No one even twitched. I was hoping for some response at least.*

"Many signals. Panicked attempts at communications. Demands that we identify ourselves. Threats for us to depart from their space."

"Ignore their chatter."

"As you command."

"The Makers have ordained this. We must cleanse this system of the tainted infidels." Dormus skittered to the display tank. "By the Celestial Egg, the mammals have polluted the entire ecosystem." Their cities had spread across the landmasses and the ugly gashes of strip-mines scarred the once-lush plains. "They corrupt all that they touch." His scales glistened moistly in the light from the array of monitors and screens. "Do they still seek to communicate with us?"

"Yes, Deacon-Prince."

"Then let us respond." His yellow eyes narrowed. "Target the main settlement." His tail twitched once.

"Target locked."

A claw-tipped hand gestured. "Cleanse them."

The *Chapel*-class battlemoon rotated slowly above the green-blue planet. It was a vast object, a central globe surrounded by lesser globes, all interconnected by interweaving tubes. Lights blinked serenely from spires and towers that jutted outwards from the spheres at odd angles. Suddenly, bursts of plasma fire streaked from their launchers and the bolts blazed ground ward.

Dormus watched the capitol city of the infidels vanish in a series of fireballs.

"The infidels have been cleansed, Deacon-Prince."

"As the Makers have commanded." Dormus lowered his head for a moment of quiet thanksgiving prayer. "We are sworn to our duty and our duty is clear. Continue to target the mammalian infestation and eradicate it."

"As you command."

"As the Makers command, Prelate."

"Of course, forgive me."

"Granted." Dormus could afford to be magnanimous. *The Makers have gifted me the chance to serve Their will. I must not fail Them.*

* * *

"Deacon-Prince, the *Divine Wrath* has broken orbit."

Dormus remained curled on the floor of his quarters. "Excellent," he hissed. Incense tickled at the scent receptors in his tongue. "The Makers are pleased with their children."

The robed and hooded acolyte remained kneeling in the posture of respect. "We do not believe there are any survivors."

"There should not be." Dormus opened his eyes abruptly.

The acolyte flinched.

"The Makers have not spoken of survivors...thus, there cannot be any."

The second robed figure finally spoke. "The crew are fulfilled with this mission's success."

"The Makers have entrusted us with a holy mission, Prelate. We must cleanse the infidels from the worlds they pollute." Those mammals with all that disgusting fur could hardly be considered intelligent creatures. They were vermin to be eradicated by the Blessed.

"Some small few do wonder if we are operating with the correct doctrine."

"Oh?" Dormus allowed his voice to be deceptively calm. *Questioning our doctrine?* he thought in outrage. *That cannot be permitted.*

The acolyte seemed unsure if he should continue. The Prelate felt no compunction about clarifying the minor debate that was being whispered in the lower decks. "Bombarding the habitations from orbit seems...wrong."

Dormus turned the full force of his gaze onto the hapless prelate. "Divine wrath or naval bombardment...it is just a matter of semantics."

"As you say, Deacon-Prince."

"The Makers speak to me. They have given their instructions to us. We must not fail Them."

"The Sword of Truth have sworn their lives—their *souls*—to the success of our jihad, Deacon-Prince."

"The Sword must not fail."

* * *

"Operatives from the Dagger of Knowledge have reported back to us about the next world."

Dormus gestured for the Acolyte to continue. He could still catch faint traces of incense on his tongue, a lingering ghost from his meditations.

"The natives call the world *Luminous Gem.*"

"Presumptive of them. We shall see how their world shines then once we have cleansed it."

"Our operatives were unable to return to the *Divine Wrath*. They remain on the surface."

Dormus nodded his understanding. "They will be blessed for their willing martyrdom," he acknowledged. All of the Sword's operatives knew the risk of spiritual contamination and material death was often the price each must pay in service to the Church. "How long until we leave hyperspace?"

"A tenth-arc."

"I will come to the bridge."

* * *

A small shudder announced the battlemoon's entry into real-space. Dormus scarcely noticed it—after years of space travel, it was commonplace to him now. "Show me this tainted world."

From orbit, the planet was barren. A desert world of reddish sand.

"There are a handful of settlements in the northern latitudes. The dominant mammalian lifeform is called *Human*. We believe they are loyal to the Republic."

"What do their secular squabbles matter to us?" Dormus demanded of the Acolyte. "Republic, Hegemony, Separatist...all are merely corrupt perversions of the truth for those who labour in ignorance of the Makers."

"Their war does have some slight advantage to us."

Dormus looked at the Prelate. "It does?" His scales itched at the thought of the mammals being useful to the Church.

"It distracts them."

The bridge was quiet.

"Without the ongoing wars, the Republic might have responded to our cleansing operations with a military venture. We might have faced battle fleets instead of these all-but-defenceless planets."

"I do not fear the Republic's battle fleet. I trust that the Sword does not fear the possibility of bitter fighting?"

"The Sword is sworn to the service of the Church. If commanded to fight, then we will fight. Should the infidels challenge us, then the Sword will smite them."

"A fine boast, Prelate. I trust that you will recall those words in due time." Domus gestured. "Lock targets on the centres of habitation."

"Targets locked. Purifier cannons are charged."

"Cleanse this world." Dormus felt his tensions drain away as the barrage began. "The Makers' will be done," he whispered.

Delusions of Grandeur

The wind whistled through Vorkuta.

Pieter Kabrinsky slowly paced through the halls of his Palace. "Kara, I trust you above all my children."

"I know, Father." She offered him a warm smile.

"Once, our world dominated every other system within hundreds of light-years. Our family commanded the obedience of billions."

"Until the Fifth Battle of Kandahar." Kara nodded as her ornate robes rustled.

"When the Republic destroyed our Conquest Fleet." That had been a crushing blow to the dreams of the Kabrinsky family...and to the Marduk Tyranny. "Now we are a dying world."

"We are not dying!" Kara protested.

"We do not prosper. We stagnate and wallow amid our decay."

"We are faring better than many systems."

An old man in jewel-encrusted body armour stepped onto the balcony with a grim smile. "Wars tear at the fabric of civilisation," he said. "The Republic has all but collapsed into chaos. Our sector remains secure."

"We have outlived our oppressors," Kara pointed out. "That should count for something."

"Not for enough." Pieter gestured to the city. "A thousand monuments to our past glories," he scoffed. "Dusty and decaying relics of a once-glorious past. Better to see the city burn than to remain in the dusty ruins. We were once rulers of the galaxy...now we are a museum display. 'Gaze at the splendour of the past now faded into memory.'"

"Never!" Kara told him with anger in her voice. "Yes, the Marduk family has bowed to the Republic—we had little choice—but I will not see our cities burn and our people die in vain."

"You have more hope than."

"She is still young."

Pieter looked at his Lord-Marshall. "You and I are of an age, Tikonov. We know what comes in the night."

"Perhaps."

Kara shook her head, exasperated with the musing of two old men. "The envoys are coming." She gestured to a star falling from the sky. "We must prepare ourselves for the conference."

* * *

The Great Hall was glorious when all the torches were lit. 'Grand barbaric splendour' was how Kara had once termed it. The long wooden tables were laden with delicacies served on golden dishes. Torchlight flickered and made shadows dance on the tapestry-hidden walls.

The Hegemony officers seemed bored by the display.

"The terms are simple," the leader—Captain Anna Nichol—smiled warmly at the Tyranny's nobles. "The taxes are quite reasonable in exchange for the benefits of being a member of the Celestial Hegemony."

"I do not see many benefits," Pieter said harshly. "I do see slavery and subservience to your Archon."

"The alternative, Marduk, is being viewed an enemy of the Hegemony and the Archon does not tolerate threats to his people."

"The Hegemony is stretched thin. You lack the military strength to wage war here."

"We could find the strength."

"I doubt that."

Kara hastily refilled her father's goblet like a dutiful daughter should while masking her tension. "Perhaps you should reconsider the terms," she suggested in a calm voice. "We are a poor sector. We lack many resources."

"You have a shipyard."

"A small one. The Republic refused to allow us to rebuild the former Yards when they absorbed our Tyranny."

"An oversight the Archon might reconsider. A strong ally in this region could be valuable."

"Indeed." Tikonov nodded.

Pieter mumbled something beneath his breath.

The stars were shining brightly.

Two Hegemony guards turned, hands resting on their sidearms.

Kara Kabrinsky smiled warmly as she stepped onto the landing pad. "A moment of your time, Captain?"

Anna Nichol nodded. "Of course, Tyrant-Heir." She gestured for the two guards to board the waiting shuttle. "Your father had few enough words for us at dinner."

Kara rested her hand on Anna's arm. "You must forgive him, Captain. My father is old and set in his ways. He has spent too many decades among these old monuments to past glories."

The Hegemony Captain nodded her understanding. "There are a lot of statues around here."

"The Tyranny ruled a vast region of space for centuries. Even before the Empyrean Republic was first founded, my family had bound together this sector under our rule."

"The Tyranny is mentioned in the histories."

"I should hope so. Our history is a proud one...as my father ages, his grief has led him into the past. I do not think his mind is fully aware of the present. The current state of the galaxy is chaotic...perhaps too confusing for him to fully grasp. The demands of politics weigh heavy on him with the ongoing Wars."

"So far you have remained neutral in the Wars."

"We lack a strong military. We lost most of our military assets during the Assimilation." *When the Republic overthrew my ancestors and occupied our worlds*, she thought bitterly. "We were never allowed to repair the infrastructure to rebuild our military."

"A pity."

"We maintain only the most basic police forces. A handful of ships to patrol our trade lanes and deal with pirates." She laughed. "Even pirates don't bother with this sector much."

"Your worlds are tapped out."

"The Marduk Sector is resource poor. That is one reason my ancestors sought to build a star-spanning empire."

"I will speak with the Archon's advisors. Perhaps you will be able to host a Fleet Anchorage out here. A Human system amid so many alien strongholds should be protected."

"Our neighbours are peaceful...they lost the will to fight centuries ago." When they had been proper servants of the Marduk family. *They knew their places back then...before the Republic sought to make us treat them as* equals.

"What of the Separatists?"

"We have had little contact with their envoys," Kara replied. "The Marduk sector is isolated...we're of little use to them."

"The Cor'vul'nin could pose a threat."

"Their confederacy is weak. We could crush it at our leisure."

"If you had the ships to spare?"

"Yes, if we had a battle fleet. For now, we merely patrol our space and make ourselves appear to dangerous to attack directly."

"Does that strategy work?"

"For now. But sooner or later, some species will challenge us and then I fear that the Tyranny will be doomed."

Anna nodded. "I must go. I have other worlds to visit on this patrol."

"Of course, Captain. I will speak with my father. Even if he refuses to ally with the Hegemony, he will not live forever. The next ruler of

Marduk might well be more *sympathetic* to your Archon's generous offer."

Anna nodded. "Good evening then."

* * *

"The *Courgeous* has reached Damascus."

"Thank you, Lord-Marshall." Kara nodded to Tikonov. "I trust that she will find nothing out of the ordinary there?"

He shook his head. "The system is bereft of traffic, as usual."

"Excellent." Kara sipped from her own goblet. "Your spies are to be commended." The array of flame-gems around the rim glistened.

"They serve me...and I serve you, Kara."

"My father is deathly ill...he should be dead before morning." Or else her *doctors* would be sent into the next world. "I want you to arrange for a suitable transport to carry me to Metropolis after my coronation."

Tikonov's brown eyes narrowed. "You plan to join the Hegemony then?"

"I plan to *use* the Hegemony. If I can convince the Archon to spend his resources in establishing a military base within this sector, then my journey to the Core Worlds will be worth the expense."

"Are you certain then?"

"Explorers in my employ have located a new star system...one previously unexplored. Antioch is rich with minerals and precious metals. The planet and its asteroid belt do not appear to ever have been mined."

"That would make it a rich prize."

"A very rich prize. A world ripe for the plundering."

"A system that could support our military industry?"

"You think as I do, General. Antioch will be the centre of a new industrial effort. One that will see the Marduk Tyranny rebuild its former strength and eventually see us expand our dominance over this sector...and possibly beyond."

"Beyond? That is a dangerous gamble."

"Success requires risk!" she snapped. "The Hegemony is weak...it lacks the Republic's millennia of history and galaxy-spanning fleets to unite its member-worlds. With the Secession Wars raging, the galaxy is in turmoil. We can use this to our advantage."

"New worlds to conquer?"

"Precisely."

"You father never saw the bigger picture."

"He lived in the past." She gestured to the towering statues. "I see the future...I see new statues and monuments to modern glories."

Lord-Marshall Tikonov bowed his head. "To your lasting health, Tyrant."

Family Honour

Laser bolts cut crimson lines through the air.

"Advancing along Kingsway North…we're taking fire!"

Richard lowered the volume on his helmet speakers as he took a deep breath. It took a fierce effort of will to leave the imagined cover of a burned-out hovercar for the dubious safety of a dry fountain basin, but he ran as fast as his armoured legs could carry him.

"Gamma-Four, swing west."

"Copy that."

Richard winced as his eyes spotted a broken statue. *Dad brought me here as a boy,* he thought. The park was once such a beautiful place of gardens and water fountains with ornately carved stone basins. Now it was mostly rubble.

"What have we done to this world?" Richard asked himself as explosions thundered in the distance. *What madness demanded that we destroy a world to save it? Where is the honour in this battle?*

"I refuse!"

"How can you just say that?"

"I'm not leaving Udon."

"But—"

"I will not leave my home."

Richard watched his parents argue. The arguments came more and more frequently these days.

"Soon Yee?"

"No, Stephen. I am staying here."

Bullets from a hidden sniper's nest stitched a path along one of the walls.

A Republican soldier dropped to the street with a grunt.

"Squad Five-Seven reporting in. Enemy armour has been neutralised. No prisoners taken."

Richard snapped off a quick shot from his rifle. He ducked back down as the sniper nest returned fire. "Gamma-Two-One here. Sniper nest located. Attempting to neutralise." Such a bloodless way of describing his intention to kill someone.

"Copy that," his commander replied. *"The rest of the squad is falling back. There's too much resistance along the western flank. We're leaving it for the aero wing."*

Richard fired towards the window he thought the sniper was using.

More bullets chewed at the wall he was hiding behind.

"I don't agree with all of the Senate's decisions, but I will not resign from my posting. I am a warrior. It's who I am, it's what I do."

"You could enlist with the Home Guard."

"With the quasi-separatist rabble you mean."

Soon Yee snorted. "You're saying that you're too good for Udon's militia?"

"I serve a higher calling."

"Bah."

"I swore an oath to the President when I put on this uniform." He brushed his fingers along the pins of rank and awards he had won. "My honour cannot be easily put aside."

"I will not move to Metropolis. That world has no soul."

"I do not ask you to move there."

"But you are going there."

"I am being transferred."

"You should remain here. Udon is your home."

"Udon is your home world. It was my posting." Stephen's tone softened. "It became my home."

"Yet you leave your family?"

"I've been reassigned to serve on one of the SpaceGuard Stations. I can't take the boys onboard the station with me. Nor would I ask them to live on Metropolis without their mother."

"I will not live on that dead world."

"Metropolis has fine gardens and parks."

"It has too much city."

"Soon, it's only for a few years. Then we can come back here."

"I will not go."

"Move towards the city's heart."

"Delta-Squad is cut off. Seps are closing on our position."

"Sniper!"

Lasers hissed overhead.

Richard glanced up as a squadron of fighters soared past. *StarHawks*, he identified them. Those aerospace fighters were Republican. So far the airspace over Udon's capitol was peaceful.

"There is talk of war."

"I know."

"Mother, I have a duty to serve."

"You have a duty to your family."

"As the firstborn son, I carry the family honour."

"Yes."

"I will join the military."

"Udon's Home Guard or the Republican Judicial Forces?" Soon Yee demanded of him.

"Udon's loyalty to the Republic is questionable."

"That does not answer my question."

"I must follow the demands of honour."

"You will obey me."

"Yes, Mother."

"I lost your father to the Republic. I won't lose you."

"You did not lose Father. You drove him away." He fell silent when his mother's hand slapped his face.

"You will not speak that way to me."

Richard stared at her.

Explosions ripped through the office block. Stone cracked and windows shattered. Shards of glass rained into the street, sending troopers scrambling for cover.

Richard reloaded his rifle with his last clip of ammo. *I hope the logistics team arrives soon,* he thought, *or else the fighting is gonna have to get really close and personal.*

An officer approached. "Report."

"The area is reasonably secure." Richard glanced around. "But I can't make any promises."

"The locals are good fighters. They're using every possible hiding place to ambush us. The price for securing this world is going to be very high."

"The Udonese are a stubborn people."

The officer shrugged. "They should never have rebelled."

Gunfire rang out.

"That's just a few streets over."

The officer gestured to his troops. "Prepare to move out. "

"Sir, we're low on ammunition."

"The supply team should be arriving shortly. You, you, you, and you remain here with me. The rest of you will establish a perimeter." He glanced around him again. "This will have to do for a command post."

Richard was the third *you* and he nodded. The corner was fairly secure and would do for an impromptu command post. Three streets came together to form a wide open space. The northern street was blocked almost completely by rubble from the buildings that had formerly stood along it. The east and south streets were still fairly clear.

The assembled troops began to move out.

More gunfire rang out.

"Rebels!" someone shouted.

Half a dozen men emerged from the rubble of the supposedly-blocked street. Their rifle shots downed half of the Republicans in seconds before return fire cut most of them down.

Breathing heavily as the gunfire stopped, Richard turned around slowly. The last Udonese native was holding a pistol towards the officer and his remaining guard.

"Surrender!" the native ordered.

"Never," the officer replied. "You will surrender to me if you want to live."

"Don't make me do this. There is no honour in cutting you down in the street."

"Do your worst."

The pistol shot took out the remaining trooper.

The officer froze as the pistol shifted back to face him.

"Honourless Rep."

"Put the gun down!" Richard shouted. He kept his own rifle aimed at the Separatist. "Now."

"You're the invader!" The Udonese man's aim didn't waver. "You have no right to order me around."

"I'm now an adult. You have no right to order me around."

Soon Yee stared at her son. "At least your brother is showing his honour in serving his home world."

"I joined the Republic Army."

"To fight against your own people?"

"Udon has not yet left the Republic," Richard pointed out. He heard the hollowness of his own words though—Udon's secession was almost certainly going to be announced any day now. "I made my choice. I swore an oath."

"You dishonour this family."

"I carry my own honour."

"Drop the gun!" Richard ordered coldly.

"No."

"Shoot him!" the officer ordered.

"Shut up!" the Udonese snapped.

"Don't make me do this," Richard begged.

"Shoot him. That's an order!"

"Shut up!" The finger of the Udonese soldier tightened on his trigger.

The officer jerked as the bullet tore into his chest, then collapsed into the dirt.

Richard fired his own rifle.

Silence seemed to fall across the entire city at that moment.

"Good shot." The Udonese crumpled.

Richard dropped his gun and stared dully at his brother's body. *At what price is honour?*

Pulling Teeth

We broke out of hyperspace as close to the planet as we could manage and dove towards Nusakan III at speed well beyond standard sublight.

Liz Jordan claimed the *Condor* could handle it.

I hoped she was right, cause the defences around Nusakan were rumoured to be strong enough to fend off an invasion.

They had proven themselves even more powerful.

The bulk of the Nusakan Star Corp had been lured to the far side of the planet, where a Hegemony battle group was attempting to land troops on the local moon. The pitched battle was too close to call, but we were betting on the Nuskies. Better firepower available to them than our frigates could give us.

The planet itself was safe enough from any flanking manoeuvres the local admiral might want to try.

That is why we were heading towards the planet at a significant fraction of lightspeed.

Admiral Sung had committed two squads of us—the Black Thorns—to this mission. We couldn't afford to fail. "Keep watching the sensors," I ordered. "If any Corps ships head this way, I want to know about them before they get into range."

"I'm on it."

We were the Black Roses, elite covert ops troops. Saboteurs.

"Massive power surge on the surface!"

"Evasive!" I snapped.

"Can't," Liz replied. "Any turns at this speed will rip us apart."

"Great."

A blinding bolt of energy stabbed from the surface, slicing through the atmosphere and lancing into space.

"Looks like the planetary defences extend to this side of the world too."

"They would have too."

A second bolt flashed past followed by a sudden glare.

"The *Dragonfly* just bought it."

"Damn." Half of our team wiped out in an instant. *This is going to make the mission even more difficult to complete.*

"We're almost to the atmosphere." Liz sounded bored. "Brace yourselves!"

Everyone grunted as the retros fired and the *Condor* slowed to a safe speed. Liz threw the ship into a curve, plunging us into the atmosphere.

"Will this bucket hold together?" I shouted over the rattle of bulkheads.

"You'll never know if it doesn't," she replied as she fought the controls.

Going in fast was our only hope to avoid being shot down.

Assuming we didn't burn up in the atmosphere or slam into the ground.

* * *

"Target Alpha."

The three members of my squad hunkered around the hologram as I displayed it for them.

"Surface-to-Space Defensive Battery Thirty-Two." Our primary target. "We have to reach it and disable it before the strike force arrives. Otherwise they die."

Our shuttle was a smouldering wreck several kilometres behind us now. We had the supplies in our packs to last us until the Hegemony could land support troops to pacify the natives.

* * *

The Battery was even more impressive in person.

It was a veritable city. The central gun rose nearly a hundred metres into the air. Lesser towers rose twenty to thirty metres in height, topped with normal laser cannon and missile launchers.

"The local defences look strong enough to fend off a pretty determined assault."

"Assuming any *StarHawks* can slip through the atmosphere, those anti-aircraft guns will make short work of them."

I scanned the Battery with my binocular implants. "No sign of obvious doors."

"I'm registering major power readings." Josh had a sophisticated sensor system implanted in his body. "They've got a fusion reactor in there strong enough to power a city."

"They need it," I agreed. The reactor was obviously underground. "Good security. No power lines to a local generator or power grid. This Battery is self-contained." According to our information, they all were.

"We need to destroy or disable this one."

That was our mission. Hegemonic Intelligence had determined that Nusakan was too strategically important to allow it to join the Separatists. Control of Nusakan would give easy access to the Lyrius Sector and its shipyards. The fact that Nusakan also produced complex computer systems added to its importance. Control of Nusakan could decide the course of the war in this region.

The drawbacks to convincing Nusakan to swear allegiance to the Hegemony stemmed from the natives' dislike of the Human-dominated Republic—and now the Hegemony that had replaced it. The other major object was the formidable planetary defences.

Like the Battery we were studying.

Nusakan had almost two hundred of the things, each one more expensive than a trio of dreadnaughts. There were advantages to a ground-based defence system of course—no one could order your defenders away to another system and leave you vulnerable being the main one. Batteries were scattered across the surface, giving overlapping fields of fire into space. No vessel could enter orbit without being the target of at least three guns.

No warship could survive more than a couple of hits.

Hence our high-speed landing during a diversionary battle.

"We have to slip in and disable that Battery." The loss of this particular Battery would open a gap in the field of fire. A small gap, true, but enough of one to allow shuttles to land their troops. Ground troops could then take control of the planet in a conventional campaign.

* * *

"The main fleet should be arriving soon." Within the hour if my internal chronometer was close to being accurate.

The turret of the huge laser cannon shifted slightly.

"I'm detecting a power surge!" Josh warned.

A bolt of green light stabbed skyward.

I blinked away the blinding light and then reeled as a thunderclap threw me to the ground. Blinking painfully, I hastily disabled my implant-enhanced senses. No sense being blinded and deafened.

"Superheated air rushing to fill the gap left by the bolt."

I knew that. "The fleet is early." Damn. I knew Admiral Sung...he had given us a few days to disable the Battery and allow the transports to ground their troops. Otherwise, he would level the planet from orbit. Orbital bombardment would cost him a few ships but once enough of the Batteries were destroyed, the cities would be vulnerable to an overwhelming reprisal.

Sung would level as many cities as he had to in order to achieve victory.

A second bolt of destructive energy stabbed upwards.

"We've got to hurry."

"I know."

Lasers were quick, but my dagger was silent.

The two guards were careless. They *knew* the enemy was still in orbit, fighting to penetrate the firepower of the Battery they were guarding. Josh and I were on them before they saw us. Both men were dead before their bodies touched the ground.

I hastily examined the door controls. A few careful connections allowed my implants to interface with the computer and override the lock. "We're in."

The corridors were quiet.

I hunkered down next to what I thought was a coolant feed.

The reactor generated a lot of heat in addition to raw energy and that was its vulnerability.

A dull hum sounded and the complex seemed to tremble as the reactor pumped obscene amounts of power to the laser emitters.

The fleet was pressing its attack, and the Battery was still in operation. Time was not on our side.

A siren began to sound.

"*I got spotted.*" Josh sounded calm as he radioed me. "*They must not remain operational.*"

"I know." I checked my equipment and set the charges.

"*Victory through service!*"

The channel went silent.

A dull thump echoed through the corridors.

We were Black Roses, sworn to serve the Archon with our lives...and our deaths.

"Intruder!" a high-pitched voice wailed.

"Damn."

Globules of plasma began to pelt the catwalk I was crouching on.

I fired a few rounds from my arm-mounted laser pistol. I didn't bother to aim, more interested in offering suppressive fire than actually killing anyone.

The defenders took cover, but continued to shoot at me.

I was exposed and vulnerable.

I could not move to another location. Most of the catwalk had been punctured and melted. I was literally being isolated. They would chip away at my cover and then kill me.

I had no choice.

The mission must come first.

"Victory through service." Our most sacred vow. Plasma splattered near my head and molten metal sprayed from the impact.

My most important implant would now be used.

The Battery could not function without the coolant feed...and as the nytro-pentum bombs within my body armed themselves, I rested against the machinery. *Victory*, I thought as a warm glow began in my chest.

What Price Security

"Soldiers on the streets," one of the men at the bar muttered a voice meant to carry across the room. "Soldiers! We used to have Judical officers and police forces. Now we have an army."

The rest of the people in the bar exchanged cautious looks.

"It's another sign of what is wrong with the Hegemony," another man finally spoke up.

"So's the fear people have to talk to each other," a woman pointed out. Her companions around the scarred table chewed at their lips.

"It is those damned aliens. Twisting and warping wholesome decent folks and turning them into monsters and traitors."

"Forget the aliens, I hate all these new taxes."

"A war is expensive to wage."

"So why wage it? If some worlds want to go off and be independent, I say *let them*!"

People shook their heads.

"I'm serious. Let some of those outer colonies try to live without access to Core technologies. Let's see how much they enjoy their vaunted *freedom* when they have no power cause their reactors are shut down and their machines are silent cause there's no spare parts. Then they'll come crawling back to us."

"That might be expensive to us as well." A grey-haired man looked up from his drink. He was seated in a shadowy corner booth, all by himself. "Without those colonies to export too, businesses will suffer from a lack of sales."

"So."

"If those desperate worlds find another source of supplies, we might lose them to some other power."

"So you're a war hawk?"

"I prefer to think of myself as a man caught up in events beyond his control. How can one stop the myriad wars now raging? They have to burn themselves out."

"The wars have cost us dearly."

"I do not deny that taxes have risen. Fighting is playing havoc with the trading routes."

"It also cost us our freedoms!" The man who had started the conversation now spoke up. "Piece by piece, law by law, we're losing the freedoms we enjoyed as citizens of the Republic."

"Surely a small enough fee for security and safety."

The woman shook her head. "The President and the Senate—"

"Are wrong."

"They paint everyone beyond the Republic as traitors."

"The Hegemony. The Republic is no more."

One dark-skinned man glared at the speaker and his fine nyax-leather jacket. "My family lives in the Grecian League, Old Man."

"A nice region...I visited New Athens on business once."

"Good for you. I was born there. My whole family is there and I've not seen nor heard from them in over two years."

Another patron shook his head. "*My* family lived on Zrezney."

The room went silent.

"Zrezney was a tragedy," the gray-haired man observed in a soft voice. He brushed at the sleeve of his maroon leather jacket. "A great tragedy."

"Indeed." The man's tone was bitter. "Seventy million dead."

An uneasy silence lasted for several minutes.

One blonde downed most of her drink. "I heard there was a protest in the Mahajan District."

"I never heard that."

"Was it on the news' casts?"

"Nope." The blonde chuckled. "Ya think the Archon is gonna let people protest his actions."

"Was the protest peaceful?" the man asked from his corner.

"Until the Muglak moved in to secure the area and disperse the crowd. Then it became a riot."

"Were you there?"

"I was on the edge."

"There was no mention of it on the news."

"I said as much. The Archon don't want no dissent being broadcast. If people heard that there was rioting in the streets of the capitol, how much more support would the Separatists gain from the Senate?"

"The Senate is a joke anymore."

"The Archon holds all the power."

"The Senate is already at half-size." So many senators had either left when their worlds seceded or else had resigned at the outbreak of the war or been arrested as traitors. "The loyalist blocks are very strong. The Archon has considerable support from them."

"Some of the Seps have stayed behind."

"I heard that."

"They're trying to maintain a sympathetic presence back in the Republic. They don't agree with the Republic's policies, but they don't want to stoke the fires of independence either."

"It won't work."

"I doubt it."

"Traitor scum."

"I heard pirates are hitting the outer colonies."

"Some of them. The Core worlds should be safe enough."

"*Should* be. They're not safe."

"Of course not. The Fleet is off fighting wars on half a dozen borders. They're not patrolling the trade routes like they used too."

"Do you think the conscription law will be passed?"

"Nope."

"Not on most planets. The Archon won't have enough support to pass that law. Not enough people are willing to enlist in the Hegemony Army."

"Rumour says the Archon has sent out spies to watch us."

"That I can believe."

"Why wouldn't he?"

"The spies failed to catch the traitors before the wars erupted. Why should they be any more effective this time around?"

"Good point."

* * *

"How was your evening, Archon?"

Tiresias smiled as he allowed his valet to remove his maroon-coloured leather jacket. "Most enlightening."

The Path Laid Out

"They're coming!"

"They're right on top of us!"

"Fall back! Fall back!"

The chatter of panicked voices echoed over the radio.

Ian Davidson winced as most of the voices went silent with ominous abruptness. "We're next on the firing line," he told his squad. "Stand by. Hold your ground." *For as long as possible*, he thought.

"The Black Fangs are closing!"

"Just what we need."

The lead line of tanks emerged from the forest.

"*Juggernauts*," Ian muttered. "Just what I didn't need to see."

Volleys of missiles erupted from the defenders and lasers stabbed at the Fangs' tanks.

Return fire gutted the defenders' ranks. Tanks were pounded into scrap and infantry were scattered and killed. The light *Scorpions* were no match at all for the heavier *Juggernauts*.

"We can't hold them!" Ian radioed to the city. "We can't stop—"

· A Pirate's Life

"Reef the sails and set course for the north star!" With a flourish of his dark blue cloak, Captain Morgan DesRoches shouted his orders. "The sun is over the yard arm!"

The crew glanced at each other.

"Which sun?" the chief helmsan asked.

"The yellow one of course." Morgan shook his head in dismay. "Show some spirit, lads. We are pirates...act like pirates!"

"Aye, Captain."

"More spirit!"

"Aye, Captain!" the crew shouted back.

"That's better." Morgan nodded his satisfaction. "Man the guns. Give them a taste of our powder."

"Laser cannon charged, Captain. We're not quite in range."

"Overtake them then. Best speed." Morgan paused a moment. "Once we're in range, give them a warning shot across their bow." He stood near the viewport and stared out across the emptiness between his ship and a richly-laden freighter.

"Coming into range now."

"Fire!" Sadly, the faint hum of power capacitors discharging lacked the raw thunder of the gunpowder-charged cannons of the wet navy warships on his distant home world. A distant flash through the view port caught his attention. He concentrated and the optic-eye patch magnified the distant freighter for him. *Damage to her hull,* he noted. "I said *across their nose*, not up it!" he shouted at the chief gunner.

"Energy spike, Captain. They're accelerating."

"The scurvy-ridden dogs are running! Full sail!"

"We want to stop them before they reach a jump point."

"I know that, Leafe."

Janis shrugged. "The *Fluttering Petal* is faster than we are. They might escape."

"Fire another shot. Disable her engines." Morgan smiled. "This is a pirate ship...we have a few surprises left."

"Energy spike!"

"What the blazes is it, Don?" Morgan bellowed.

"Warship coming out of hyperspace!"

"Damn." He adjusted his eye-patch. *Hegemony frigate...we're outgunned.* "Alter course! Hard to port! Gunners, fire at will."

"Aye, Captain."

"Captain?"

"Not now, Saunders."

"Transponder beacon reads as *Blinding Vengeance*."

"*Fluttering Petal* has jumped to hyperspace."

Gone from my grasp. Damn. Morgan cursed loudly—mostly because it was expected of the image he sought to project. "Fire a broadside at them."

"Aye, Captain."

"The frigate is closing."

"Full power to the screens." Morgan felt his ship shudder as energy bolts splattered against the defence screens. "Return fire!" Again, he missed the thunderous boom of his cannon.

"We're being ordered to stand down."

Morgan didn't reply.

"Captain?"

"I shall reply from the mouth of my cannon," Morgan declared rather arrogantly. "Alter course bearing two three mark five. Full speed."

"That takes us right at them."

"I know."

"A collision course?"

"They'll blink first."

"Engines charged...we can jump to hyperspace at your command."

"Thank you, Jenkins." He stared at the frigate. "They'll blink first." Weapons' fire splattered the screens and his own cannon replied. *I don't think we're even scratching their paint,* he thought.

* * *

Grey Soul Station was one of the galaxy's infamous shadow ports. It was a space station, which operated as a free port outside of the law. The Republic had sought to shut the port down repeatedly and failed every single time. In part, the safety was due to Grey Soul having a hyperdrive installed at its core that allowed the station to vanish into hyperspace whenever Judicial Forces ships ventured too close. The other protection came from the Senate, many of whose members relied on the port for special missions of their own.

"So, is the *Crimson Claw* ready for the scrap yard?"

"Not yet, Borloosh."

The grey-scaled Portmaster shrugged. "Pity...I could give good price."

"Talk to Leafe. We need a few repairs...and some upgrades."

"Not cheap."

"There's a war on," Morgan grumbled. "Every system in the galaxy is suddenly full of warships and they all shoot first." He grunted. "It's not *fun* being a pirate anymore."

"The collapse of the Republic good for business."

"The rise of the Hegemony is not. These new Army and Fleet officers are more dangerous than the Judicials ever were. The Archon has given them orders to shoot first and take no prisoners."

"The Fleet is stretched then."

"True. That is the only saving grace."

"Weapon upgrades?"

"Yes. Engines need to be tuned. Change the harmonics and *see* if that will give me more speed."

"I do what I can."

The bar was crowded with beings in various stages of intoxication.

Morgan had only just gotten a mug of Tauran ale when he was jostled by two hulking Mugruts trying to beat each other senseless. The bar's bouncers quickly subdued the two felonoids and threw them out. "Kara!"

The blonde smiled, the expression marred by the tug of the scar on her right cheek. "Morgan, you old snive-rat. What brings you to Grey Soul?"

"Some upgrades to the *Claw*."

"Got smoked in a fight?"

"We gave as good as we got. The Hegemony has a frigate in for repairs right now too."

"The Separatists will love you for that."

"I have no love for them...but their treasure is as nice to plunder as any." He flourished his cloak.

"Maybe they can get you a new hat." Kara snorted. "That plume is absurd.

"I rather like it."

"You are in love with the ideals of piracy."

"I am in love with the wealth which comes from the act of piracy."

"There are other ways to make money."

"Work?" Morgan gasped. "Menial labour?"

"You're right, what was I thinking?"

"I've never done an honest day's work in my life. No fun in it."

"No fun in getting your atoms scattered across a star system."

"True."

"Privateering."

"What of it?"

"It's more popular now. The Separatists and the Hegemony are both struggling to get more naval strength. The recent campaigns in the Winespring and Caledonian Sectors have drained both sides."

"The Caledonian Sector is fully pacified though...the Hegemony crushed the independence movements there." He had little love for the Hegemony—or for the Republic that had spawned it—but the Separatists were little better.

"The Hegemony is at less than thirty per cent strength in that sector. If the KungesArmy could muster some ships, they could take the sector capitol with little effort. If the Hegemony tries to hold Caledonia, the KungesArmy could claim a dozen other worlds easily."

"But they both lack ships."

"Precisely." Kara sipped from her mug. "Which is likely why Zwadski has come to Grey Soul."

"A Separatist leader here?"

"And a Hegemony officer a well. Wingmaster Tweesk, I think was the name."

"Both of them here?"

"Grey Soul will be jumping after they leave. We're in no danger."

"So you say."

"They both made generous offers for ships to join their cause.

"How generous?"

"Tweesk offers a full pardon from the Archon for any criminal acts we might have previously committed. Standard fleet wages, plus a thirty per cent bonus for combat."

"Payable after the tour of duty ends?"

"Of course."

"And what do the Separatists offer?"

"This group are offering a flat bounty on any ships destroyed or captured. Fifty per cent purchase for destroyed and one hundred per cent purchase for captured ships."

They would use captured ships to bulk up their own fleets...clever. Weaken their enemy and increase their own strength at the same time. "Seems generous enough."

"The shipyards are heavily committed to building warships. Neither side can get enough ships."

"I heard rumours of Hegemony ships massing near the Fokkers-Mitsubishi Yards."

"I heard the same rumours."

"You said that Zwadski was only 'this group' of Separatists. There are others?"

"Of course." One of the Separatist failings was that so many groups had declared their independence from the faltering Republic at the same time, but they did not unify into a new political block. They maintained some trade ties, but their interactions were short of a full alliance.

"What was their offer?"

"The Grecian League offers a landhold in exchange for pledging allegiance to their cause."

"No thank you. I have no desire to become part of their political struggles." Each planet was all but independent of the others...an alliance of city-states on an interstellar scale. "I like my independence." He raised his mug. "Too piracy."

Kara smiled and raised her own mug.

"Don't you think that using the *Claw's* firepower to blast a freighter into debris because its captain wouldn't surrender to you was overkill?"

"There is no such thing as *overkill*," Morgan replied calmly. "There is only *open fire* and *I need to reload*." He took another drink. "No other captain in that system resisted me after that display."

"I heard that too. I also heard that you were asked to join the KungsArme against an Arcadian Patrol. An alliance of mutual convenience?"

"The enemy of my enemy?"

"Is still my enemy," Kara finished.

"I'm a pirate, not a fool. First you pillage *then* you burn, etc." He laughed. "Someone should write a book about the habits of successful pirates."

Both captains laughed.

Insects

Jorgan dropped to the ground as artillery shells fell on the lower slopes of the ridge. "I hate this!" he wailed.

The artillery barrage slackened.

"Is it over?"

"What did we do to deserve this?" Dokal shouted back. "We could be home fishing right now."

"We volunteered to defend the Hegemony."

"Instead we're getting pounded from orbit!"

Jorgan sighed. "This is my first trip off-world."

"It might be your last." Dokal checked her rifle. "Are those droids?"

"Where?" Jorgan looked. "Ye gods," he moaned.

Hundreds of metallic forms were striding across the grassy field towards the ridge.

Hegemony soldiers, so much taller and more impressive than the two diminutive Frella, hefted their own weapons. Armoured vehicles and support-class weapons took aim.

"Fire for effect!" one of the Humans bellowed.

Explosions tore at the robotic ranks. Numerous machines blew apart in thunderous clouds of metallic shrapnel.

Return fire stabbed at the Hegemony positions.

"It's almost pretty," Jorgan commented. Bolts of multi-coloured light stabbed through the air. Missiles left scores of smoky contrails. Explosions cast flashes of light across the field.

"We are so dead," Dokal said as she stared down at the approaching war-droids. "They're not stopping!"

"I thought we could hold. The captain said we would hold." Jorgan looked around to complain. "I never enlisted to get killed on some gods-forsaken rock."

A *Scorpion* tank was hit and blew apart, throwing a portion of the defensive line into chaos.

The two Frella ducked and rolled under the legs of one spider-like droid. The machine never seemed to notice them, intent on destroying a Hegemony tank.

"We're out of our depth!" Dokal shouted over the roar of weapons' fire.

"I know," Jorgan agreed. The Humans were retreating, and their legs were allowing them to run faster than the Frella. "Wait for us!"

Several tanks were in retreat, firing as they moved.

"We're being ignored!"

"Is that a bad thing?"

"Maybe not." Jorgan looked around. The battle—once so organized—was now chaos. "We're getting our butts kicked." The Hegemony was in full retreat.

"Are we losing?"

"We've lost." Jorgan stared at one of the towering war-droids. "We give up!"

The droid moved past him without slowing its lumbering steps.

"We're still being ignored."

"How embarrassing. We can't even surrender."

"We need an organic commander."

"I know."

"We're like insects to them. Ignored by both sides."

"Maybe we can sting them...get noticed then."

"Got any ideas?"

Dokal hefted her rifle. "Points for hitting those druids?"

"You're on."

Supreme Heights

Mooga Chas, Sirdar of the Sigma Supremacy, paced calmly through the square towards the Citadel. Here, in the capitol of the Supremacy, she feared no enemy.

The Citadel loomed before her. It was the most imposing structure in the sector, designed to symbolise the Supremacy's confidence and belief in its own superiority. Such aspirations were made by the gleaming marble and glass five-sided of which the ziggurat was composed. Tall spires rising from each corner and from the highest peak. The vast majority of the Citadel's weapon turrets were camouflaged—their very existence a rumour.

"Hail, Sirdar."

"Hail, TalonMaster."

The tall officer rippled his fur. "I trust you slept well."

"I did. How fares the battle?"

"The Hegemonics have withdrawn from Sigma Draconis. They lost many ships and warriors in that failure."

"They will send others."

"Sirdar, we are strong."

"So are they." Mooga sighed. "The Supremacy must be held! I will not see our worlds defiled by any other power."

"The Celestial Hegemony is no greater than the Republic. We can hold our own."

"I trust that is so...for your sake."

"Sirdar, we have taken many worlds in this war. We will hold them...despite raids from the former Republic."

"We were the first to declare ourselves free of the dying Republic...we will not be forced into rejoining the Hegemony now."

"I quite agree."

"Then what must we do?"

"The shipyards labour at their best to expand our fleet. I suggest leaving them to do so. Victory will come then when we deploy fleets that outnumber the very stars. The Supremacy will not falter."

· **The Time Of Unity**

"The Hew-Monon have gone too far."

"What have they done this time, Seeker?"

"They have profaned the golden sands of Kai'Lokan with their presence." The Seeker failed to mask the shudder that shivered through him at the thoughts of the paths of the holy shrines being walked upon by the Hew-Monon.

"What can we do?"

"What we must." The Seeker raised his head. "We will do what we must."

* * *

"It is time to unleash the arms of the ancients." Seeker Lerous stared the enclave. "We must take these steps to defend our dwindling worlds."

"We are a race in decline, Seeker." One of the Clan Elders made that statement in a calm voice. "What hopes have we of making a serious challenge to the Youngling Races?"

"You would have us step aside and be lost in the mists of history?" Lerous demanded. "Once, our race strode through the stars like giants. Our civilisation flourished on the worlds beneath a million stars."

"And now we possess only a handful of our ancient homes."

"We decline."

"The Younglings rise."

"The Hew-Monon spread like vermin."

"We cannot war with them all."

"We can defend what we possess. We can take back those worlds we once deemed vial."

"Our numbers dwindle...the Younglings multiply."

"The Younglings war with one another."

"Barbarians."

"This is our time to use such knowledge as we possess...they have numbers greater than the stars themselves, but they squander that strength with their current foolishness. This is the chance we have waited for...this is the time for us to retake our lost worlds."

"We have the ancient sciences. We can use them to once again master the stars."

* * *

"The work of our shaping is a delicate task, Seeker. The songs cannot be rushed else the work will not be pure."

"I applaud your skills, Shaper." Lerous stood on the hilltop, looking down into the valley. The Shapers were labouring, singing their songs and crafting the first of his *Shrikes*. The morning light caught the crystalline hull and shone with a thousand colours. "They are works of beauty." They would look like living creatures gliding through the void of space.

"It is difficult work...a single craft requires much effort and talent to shape."

"You will provide me with what you can...I will spend our resources sparingly."

* * *

"You are set upon this course?"

"I am."

"Violence is not the answer."

"It is the only language the Hew-Monon truly understand." Such a primitive barbaric species...and yet they ruled so much of what the Race had once inhabited. "Our worlds are lost...I will not see their surfaces profaned by the presence of such primitive beings."

"Are you certain of this course of action?"

"Would you leave the sacred worlds to the Hew-Monon?"

"We have avoided dealings with them for centuries. They do not even remember our existence."

"We are legends to them now...it is time for legends to once again walk among the stars."

* * *

"The *Guardian* stands ready."

Lerous nodded. "Then it begins." He gestured sedately. "Guide, open the pathway."

Kernos waved his hand above his instruments. The translucent green crystal shimmered with inner light and chimes tinkled softly. "The path is visible to me, Seeker."

"Then take us down it."

The crystalline structure of the ship resonated as the craft phased out of normal space and into the realm of the Beyond.

* * *

"We near Kai'Sorich."

"What of the Hew-Monon?"

"I sense their vessels."

"Show me." Lerous watched a patch of wall shimmer and reveal a visual image of the reddish planet. "Kai'Sorich...it has been long since any of us walked your moist sands." Two objects glinted in orbit. "Enhance them." The image focused on the two ships. "They are Hew-Monon." There was no mistaking the blocky, harshly mechanical lines of the Hew-Monon vessels.

"We sense a settlement on the surface."

"First we must deal with those corvettes." *Babylonian*-class, he believed the Hew-Monon called them in their unlovely language. "Take us forward."

"The Hew-Monon have seen us. They are attempting contact."

"Ignore them, Singer. Their grunting holds no interest for me." He watched the two vessels growing larger on the display. "Claw them."

One of his crew waved his hand above his panel, then clenched his fist.

A hum resonated through the ship.

A laser stabbed out and burned into the lead warship. The block engine bank was severed from the rest of the fuselage.

"They are continuing to chatter at us."

"Let them hear my words." Lerous paused while the songmaster adjusted the transmission systems. "We are the hand of vengeance," he said in the dominant Hew-Monon language. "We come to reclaim all that was once ours. We will rule what we once ruled. Our time has come again." The lead Hew-Monon corvette blew apart. "Disable the other one," he ordered calmly. "They will call for aid and more of them will come."

"Do we fight on?"

"No. This is the first of our *Guardians*. I will not risk it in a battle until it has been tested further." The second Hew-Monon vessel had been disabled by the barrage. "Take us into orbit."

* * *

"You were successful, Seeker?"

"A surprise strike against a lightly defended outpost held little challenge."

"Little honour as well."

"Honour has a place, but sometimes a warrior must sacrifice his honour for the betterment of his people."

"You destroyed one corvette, disabled the other, and then levelled the entire settlement."

"The Hew-Monon have learned to fear us."

"They will not be pleased."

"They will fight."

"They will lose any war they start. My single ship proved far superior to the pair of them."

"Your *Guardian* is a powerful ship. It was an unfair fight."

"I did what I must." Lerous shook his head. "I will continue to do what I must to safeguard our people."

The Hidden Cost

"You can see the devastation from here."

"Yes, it's quite...extensive."

The shuttle banked.

"You can track the course of the war from the path of damage," Kerous said. "The planet has been fought over extensively."

"You were the first world to throw off the shackles of the long-decaying Republic."

"Brittany's first and only claim to galactic fame." Kerous shook his multiple limbs. "A street riot erupted against the Trade Conglomerate. Taxation riots, it seemed, were the order of the day and the Republic's judicial forces were unable to secure the streets. Our citizens fought their way into the spaceport and seized it."

Most of the central complex was a crater.

"The Republic counterattack was fierce."

"Understatement, if I ever heard one."

"Orbital bombardment by Clawmaster Zgrek. The attack destroyed two cities on the southern continent. He sent in assault shuttles with support fire. The spaceport was a priority target...and after his fourth attack wave was shot down, he had the port razed."

"If I recall the reports, your militia was using the port as its command centre."

"True."

The shuttle soared past the edge of the capitol. Rubble choked the streets, evidence of fought-over buildings. Destroyed tanks and vehicles still stood where they had been destroyed and abandoned.

"Republican troops forced their way into the city, despite our strongest efforts. It took them weeks to secure the outer suburbs. Weeks and hundreds of lives."

"What's that metallic river?"

"The war-droids."

"War-droids?"

"Some of our secessionist allies sought to aid us. Their droids fought past the warship blockade and landed ground forces. The fighting lasted three weeks before the last Republican outpost fell."

"You took few prisoners."

"A mistake on our part. The war-droids were not programmed to take prisoners and they attacked with a relentlessness we had not considered." Kerous shook his head. "The price we paid for that error...."

"Republic counterattack?"

"Their fleet smashed the Separatist KungsArme squadron and laid down orbital bombardment on every war-droid concentration they could detect. None of their commanders worried about civilians caught in the cross-fire."

"The war was turning us all into animals."

"Small wonder we fell into a civil war."

"That I had not heard about."

"No? By then Brittany was no longer important to your Republic. Your Archon was trying to rally his fading support by renaming his stellar empire. His military forces were withdrawn and thrown against other targets. More strategic worlds. Planets with tactical importance or vital resources. Brittany was left for its own citizens to fight over."

"More suffering, more misery."

"The pro-Hegemony faction won."

"For a time. For a few months we knew an uneasy peace." Kerous allowed the shuttle to hover over a shattered building complex. "Then the KungsArme returned and sought to impose its will on us. Force us to join their alliance and continue the fight against the Hegemony."

"You fought back."

"And we lost."

"Then the Archon remembered you and sent his Hegemonic Navy to rescue you."

Kerous bared his fangs. "We still do not know which faction detonated the biochemical warheads."

Commander Kimball-Holland chewed at her lip. "Nor do we." She adjusted her uniform tunic. "The Archon gave no order to render the planet uninhabitable."

"Brittany is still poisoned. The atmosphere is tainted with a biochemical soup we are still trying to analyze."

"The study is being taken over by Hegemony scientists."

"So the findings can be lost?"

"The truth will be known."

"Our world is dying. Our people are dying."

"The spoils of war." Commander Kimball-Holland eyed the city with a twist to her mouth. "A fine example for other worlds considering rebellion against the Hegemony."

Connect with Me Online:

Smashwords:
http://www.smashwords.com/profile/
view/MattKirkby

Follow on Twitter—
https://twitter.com/talonspiritcat

Facebook: http://facebook.com/
MattKirkby

Also by Matt Kirkby

A Novel of Lovecraftian Horror
The Death of Hope

Stories Of Feudal Japan
With Honour Veiled

The Empyrean Republic
The Price To Be Paid
The High Cost Of Victory
Empress of All The Stars

Standalone
A Wyrm In the Heart
Cthonian Dragons
Forlorn Gambit
Reap What Has Been Sown
The Horror From The Sea
Vector Of Infection

About the Author

Born and raised in small-town Ontario, Matt Kirkby is a romantic dreamer who specializes in writing tales of high fantasy and pulp-style science fiction and space operas. He draws his inspiration from all diverse sources and ideas: Science Fiction, Fantasy, Gothic Horror, Pastoral Nature. He started his writing career submitting fan fiction for numerous Star Wars and TransFormers fanzines, but has since moved on to writing professionally. He published his first novel, A Wyrm In The Heart in 2004. He lives a double life, writing classy sci-fi and fantasy for fun under his own name, and penning gay erotica under the pen name of Frank Sol. When not writing, Matt spends his time helping his partner with his hand-crafted rocking chair business -- www.OffYourRocker.ca -- and trying to maintain some control over his cat. He still thinks that no gift is better than a new book.